Anti-Bullying

Editor: Danielle Lobban

Volume 450

First published by Independence Educational Publishers

The Studio, High Green

Great Shelford

Cambridge CB22 5EG

England

© Independence 2024

Copyright

This book is sold subject to the condition that it shall not,
by way of trade or otherwise, be lent, resold, hired out or otherwise
circulated in any form of binding or cover other than that in which it
is published without the publisher's prior consent.

Photocopy licence

The material in this book is protected by copyright. However, the
purchaser is free to make multiple copies of particular articles for instructional
purposes for immediate use within the purchasing institution.
Making copies of the entire book is not permitted.

ISBN-13: 978 1 86168 910 8

Printed in Great Britain

Pureprint Group

Acknowledgements

The publisher is grateful for permission to reproduce the material in this book. While every care has been taken to trace and acknowledge copyright, the publisher tenders its apology for any accidental infringement or where copyright has proved untraceable. The publisher would be pleased to come to a suitable arrangement in any such case with the rightful owner.

The material reproduced in **issues** books is provided as an educational resource only. The views, opinions and information contained within reprinted material in **issues** books do not necessarily represent those of Independence Educational Publishers and its employees.

Although every effort has been made to ensure that website addresses are correct at time of going to press, Independence Educational Publishers cannot be held responsible for the content of any website mentioned in this book.

Images

Cover image courtesy of iStock. All other images courtesy of Freepik, Pixabay, Pexels, and Unsplash.

Additional acknowledgements

With thanks to the Independence team: Janey Hills, Klaudia Sommer and Jackie Staines.

Danielle Lobban

Cambridge, October 2024

Contents

Chapter 1: About Bullying

Understanding bullying	1
What is bullying?	2
What are the different types of bullying?	4
Prevalence of bullying	5
The majority of Britons have been bullied – and it had a significant impact on most	6
Bullying and online experiences among children	9
Six reasons people become bullies	12

Chapter 2: Effects of Bullying

How bullying harms the brain	14
'There's a lot of places where you can't be seen': how bullying can be invisible to adults	16
Suffering PTSD from school bullying: My search for validation	18
Could you forgive your childhood bully? Katy Wix confronts a painful memory	22
I will never forgive my school bullies – that would only help them, not me	24
From friendship to fear: my journey through school bullying and its lasting impact	26
Can bullying cause anxiety disorders?	28
Devastating effects of bullying on children in the short and long-term	30
Study finds childhood bullying linked to distrust and mental health problems in adolescence	31
Life after workplace bullying	32
Being bullied as an adult: breaking the silence	34

Chapter 3: Stamping Out Bullying

Top 5 tips to handle bullying	35
I'm a bully – and I want to stop	36
How to stop bullying others: 7 practical tips	37
Scientists find 'potential breakthrough' to stop bullying in schools	38
Stamping out bullying	39
What should I do if I'm being bullied?	40

Where can I find help?	41
Further Reading/Useful Websites	42
Glossary	43
Index	44

Introduction

Anti-Bullying is volume 450 in the **issues** series. The aim of the series is to offer current, diverse information about important issues in our world, from a UK perspective.

About *Anti-Bullying*

One in two children experience bullying in the UK. With social media, many people have no escape from their bullies. This book looks at statistics around bullying, its impact on victims and how bullying can be prevented.

Our sources

Titles in the **issues** series are designed to function as educational resource books, providing a balanced overview of a specific subject.

The information in our books is comprised of facts, articles and opinions from many different sources, including:

- Newspaper reports and opinion pieces
- Website factsheets
- Magazine and journal articles
- Statistics and surveys
- Government reports
- Literature from special interest groups.

A note on critical evaluation

Because the information reprinted here is from a number of different sources, readers should bear in mind the origin of the text and whether the source is likely to have a particular bias when presenting information (or when conducting their research). It is hoped that, as you read about the many aspects of the issues explored in this book, you will critically evaluate the information presented.

It is important that you decide whether you are being presented with facts or opinions. Does the writer give a biased or unbiased report? If an opinion is being expressed, do you agree with the writer? Is there potential bias to the 'facts' or statistics behind an article?

Activities

Throughout this book, you will find a selection of assignments and activities designed to help you engage with the articles you have been reading and to explore your own opinions. Some tasks will take longer than others and there is a mixture of design, writing and research-based activities that you can complete alone or in a group.

Further research

At the end of each article we have listed its source and a website that you can visit if you would like to conduct your own research. Please remember to critically evaluate any sources that you consult and consider whether the information you are viewing is accurate and unbiased.

Issues Online

The **issues** series of books is complemented by our online resource, issuesonline.co.uk

On the Issues Online website you will find a wealth of information, covering over 75 topics, to support the PSHE and RSE curriculum.

Why Issues Online?

Researching a topic? Issues Online is the best place to start for...

Librarians

Issues Online is an essential tool for librarians: feel confident you are signposting safe, reliable, user-friendly online resources to students and teaching staff alike. We provide multi-user concurrent access, so no waiting around for another student to finish with a resource. Issues Online also provides FREE downloadable posters for your shelf/wall/table displays.

Teachers

Issues Online is an ideal resource for lesson planning, inspiring lively debate in class, and setting lessons and homework tasks.

Our accessible, engaging content helps deepen students' knowledge, promotes critical thinking, and develops independent learning skills.

Issues Online saves precious preparation time. We wade through the wealth of material on the internet to filter the best quality, most relevant and up-to-date information you need to start exploring a topic.

Our carefully selected, balanced content presents an overview and insight into each topic from a variety of sources and viewpoints.

Students

Issues Online is designed to support your studies in a broad range of topics, particularly social issues relevant to young people today.

There are thousands of articles, statistics and infographs instantly available to help you with homework, research, and assignments.

With 24/7 access using the powerful Algolia search system, you can find relevant information quickly, easily and safely anytime from your laptop, tablet or smartphone, in class or at home.

Visit issuesonline.co.uk to find out more!

Chapter 1: About Bullying

Understanding bullying

Have you ever felt targeted, laughed at for no reason, or excluded by your peers? Bullying is more common than many think, impacting millions of teens around the world every day. It's not just about the occasional teasing; bullying can lead to serious emotional, physical, and mental health issues. Let's dive deep into understanding bullying, its effects, and how we can combat it together.

What is bullying?

Bullying is when someone repeatedly and intentionally uses words or actions against someone else to hurt or intimidate them. This can take many forms – verbal bullying includes teasing, name-calling, or making inappropriate comments. Physical bullying involves hitting, pushing, or any use of physical aggression. Cyberbullying happens online and includes sending mean texts, emails, or posting hurtful comments and pictures. A common factor in all these types is the presence of a power imbalance, where the bully holds more power, physically or socially, over the victim.

Effects of bullying

Bullying doesn't just affect the victim; it impacts everyone involved. Victims may experience depression, anxiety, and even physical symptoms like headaches and stomach aches. Bullies themselves can also face long-term emotional issues and are more likely to engage in negative behaviours such as substance abuse or delinquency. Bystanders, those who witness bullying but aren't directly involved, might feel powerless or guilty for not intervening

How to recognise bullying

Recognising bullying is the first step towards stopping it. Signs include unexplained injuries, lost or destroyed belongings, frequent headaches or stomach-aches, changes in eating habits, and avoidance of social situations. Encourage teens to talk about their experiences and remind them it's okay to reach out to adults – teachers, parents, counsellors – for help

Preventing and addressing bullying

Preventing bullying starts with creating a culture of kindness and respect.

Here are some strategies:

- Encourage empathy: Helping teens understand and empathise with others can prevent bullying behaviours.
- Promote bystander intervention: Empower teens to stand up against bullying when they see it. Sometimes, just the presence of a peer can stop a bully in their tracks.
- Seek support: Schools offer resources and support for those experiencing bullying. Don't be afraid to reach out.

In the digital age, cyberbullying can be challenging to escape. Encourage teens to keep personal information private, think before they post, and use privacy settings on social media.

Conclusion

Bullying is a serious issue, but by understanding what it is, recognising the signs, and knowing how to address it, we can all contribute to a safer, more inclusive environment for teens. Let's not stand by – stand up, speak out, and support each other to put an end to bullying.

Remember, promoting kindness and empathy starts with us. Let's make a pledge to be the change we wish to see, ensuring a brighter, bully-free future for all.

What is bullying?

Bullying is a harmful behaviour that can affect anyone, especially young people. It often involves repeated actions that hurt, embarrass, or intimidate the person being targeted. In many cases, bullying can occur in schools, online, or even at home, taking many forms such as physical aggression, verbal abuse, or exclusion. While the impact of bullying can be devastating, understanding what it is, how it works, and how to stop it can make a huge difference. This article will explore what bullying is and address some key questions surrounding it.

Is it intentional?

One of the defining features of bullying is that it's usually intentional. When someone bullies another person, they are often fully aware of their actions and the harm they are causing. The intention can range from wanting to make someone feel powerless to creating a situation where the person being bullied feels scared or humiliated.

Intentional bullying can be direct, like hitting, name-calling, or spreading rumours, or indirect, such as excluding someone from a group or gossiping about them. Whether it's verbal, physical, or emotional, the underlying goal is often to hurt or control someone else.

But it's important to distinguish between actions that are intentionally hurtful and those that are not. Sometimes people might say something mean without realising how much it affects the other person. If it's a one-time occurrence and the person apologises or changes their behaviour, it might not be considered bullying. However, when the harmful behaviour continues intentionally, it fits the definition of bullying.

Does it have to be persistent?

While bullying is often persistent, it doesn't always have to be. Persistent bullying refers to harmful actions that occur repeatedly over time. These ongoing actions create a pattern of behaviour that makes the person being bullied feel as though there is no escape. Examples include a classmate regularly teasing another student, repeatedly pushing or hitting them, or continually spreading negative rumours about them. This form of bullying is the most commonly recognised because it has a cumulative effect, increasing stress and anxiety in the victim as the behaviour continues.

However, not all bullying has to be persistent to have a harmful impact. Sometimes a single, severe incident can be just as damaging, particularly if it involves violence,

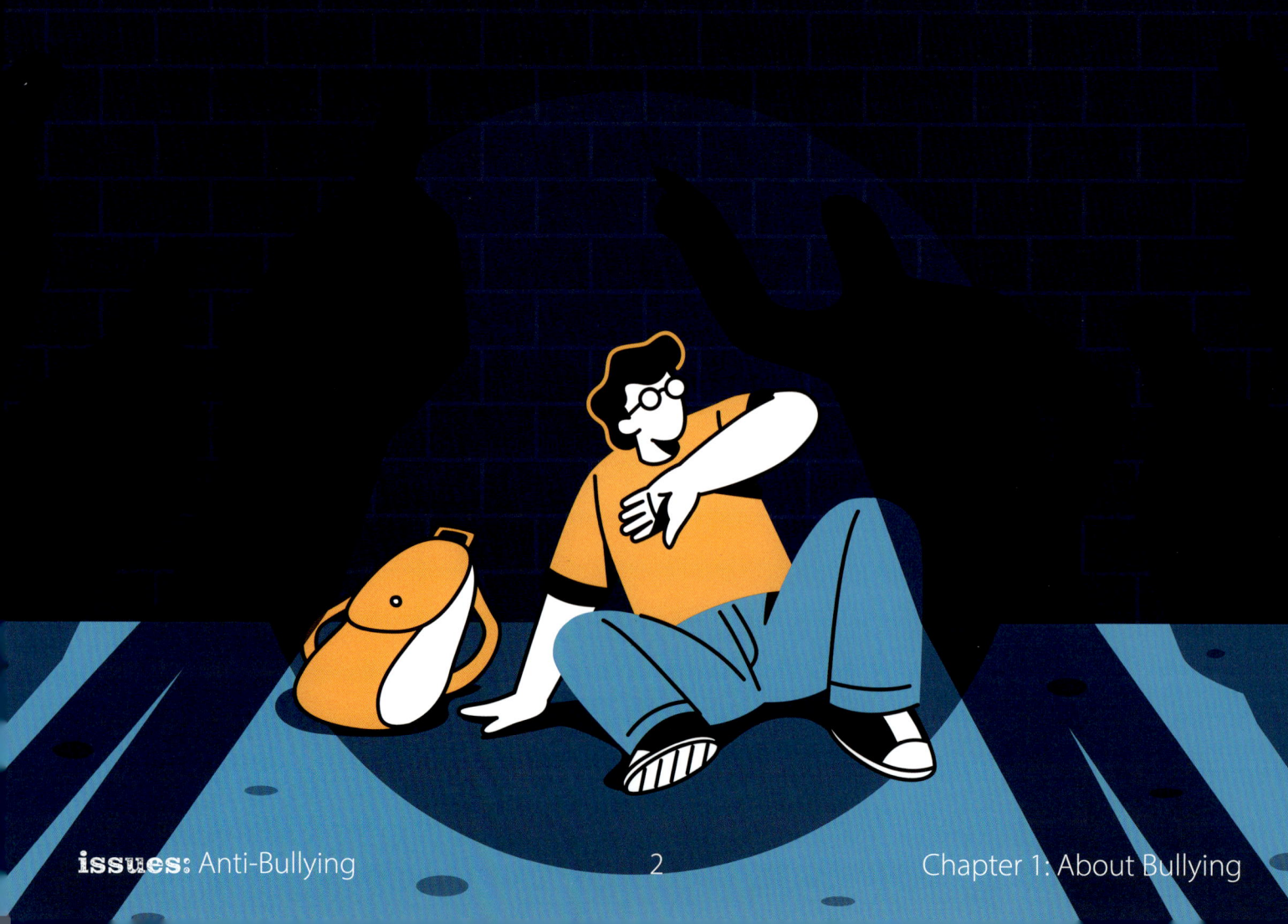

significant threats, or a major public embarrassment. These incidents can cause immediate harm and long-lasting effects on a person's confidence or mental health, even if they don't happen repeatedly. This is why it's important to understand that bullying isn't just about repetition; it's about the intent and the impact of the behaviour, whether it happens once or many times.

Is it always bullying?

It's normal for young people to have disagreements or arguments with friends, family members, or classmates. Sometimes people say things in the heat of the moment or make mistakes, but this doesn't always mean it's bullying. So how can you tell the difference?

Bullying tends to involve an imbalance of power. The bully is often trying to dominate or control the other person, while the person being bullied feels powerless to stop it. It's one-sided, where one person consistently tries to hurt, intimidate, or upset the other. In contrast, disagreements between friends usually involve both people expressing their opinions or frustrations, and although feelings might get hurt, the intention is not to harm or control the other person.

For example, if two classmates have a one-off argument or disagreement and then make up afterward, that's not bullying. But if one student regularly insults or threatens the other with the goal of making them feel bad, that would likely be considered bullying. Context and consistency are key factors to consider when identifying bullying behaviour.

What is online bullying?

With the rise of social media, bullying has found a new platform: the internet. Online bullying, or cyberbullying, involves using digital platforms to harass, threaten, or humiliate others. This can include sending cruel or hurtful messages, spreading false information, or sharing private images without permission.

Online bullying is particularly harmful because it can happen at any time, even when the victim is in the safety of their own home. Cyberbullying can also reach a much larger audience than face-to-face bullying, as content shared online can be seen by hundreds or even thousands of people. Additionally, the anonymity of the internet makes it easier for bullies to attack others without revealing their identities, which can make the victim feel even more vulnerable and isolated.

Another unique aspect of online bullying is that it can follow the victim everywhere. Unlike bullying at school, where the person being bullied might be able to escape the situation by going home or changing classrooms, online bullying can occur constantly, even when the victim is at home or away from school. This relentless nature of cyberbullying makes it especially damaging to the mental health and wellbeing of young people.

Design

Create a poster to highlight the issue of bullying.

Write

Write a one-paragraph definition of bullying.

Debate

Currently, in the UK there is no legal definition of bullying.

As a class debate whether there should be a legal definition or not. Half of the class will be for a legal definition, and the other half against.

What is the impact?

The effects of bullying can be severe and long-lasting, impacting both the person being bullied and the person doing the bullying. For the person being targeted, bullying can lead to emotional and psychological distress. It can cause feelings of sadness, anxiety, loneliness, and depression. In some cases, victims of bullying may withdraw from school or social situations to avoid further harassment, which can have a negative impact on their education and relationships.

Over time, bullying can erode a person's self-esteem and confidence. In extreme cases, persistent bullying can lead to more serious mental health issues such as self-harm, eating disorders, or thoughts of suicide. The impact is not just limited to the short term; victims of bullying may struggle with trust and relationships even into adulthood, as the emotional scars from their experiences may linger.

Interestingly, bullying also has an impact on the bully themselves. Research shows that those who engage in bullying behaviour are more likely to experience difficulties in forming healthy relationships later in life. They may also face disciplinary actions at school or even legal consequences, depending on the severity of their actions. Without intervention, bullies may continue to engage in harmful behaviours, affecting their future prospects and mental wellbeing.

Bullying is a complex issue that can have a deep and lasting impact on both the victims and the bullies. Whether it's intentional, persistent, or occurs online, it can seriously affect a person's emotional, mental, and social wellbeing. By recognising the signs and understanding what bullying looks like, we can take steps to stop it and create a more positive environment for everyone. If you or someone you know is being bullied, it's important to speak up. Help is available, and no one should have to face bullying alone.

What are the different types of bullying?

Bullying is a term we've all heard, and, sadly, something many of us have experienced in one form or another. It's not just a playground issue – it can follow us into adulthood and morph into new, equally damaging forms. Let's dive into the different types of bullying, their impacts, and how they manifest in our lives.

Physical bullying

Physical bullying is perhaps the most obvious form – it's all about using physical actions to gain power over someone. This could be hitting, kicking, pinching, or any other form of physical aggression. It's not just about inflicting pain; it's about instilling fear. Victims might find themselves dreading school, feeling unsafe in certain spaces, or carrying the physical and emotional scars of their experiences. Physical bullying often requires immediate intervention to ensure everyone's safety.

Verbal bullying

Words can cut deeper than we think. Verbal bullying uses language to belittle, demean, or intimidate. This could be through name-calling, insults, sexist, racist, or homophobic slurs, or any form of derogatory language aimed at eroding a person's self-esteem. The impact of verbal bullying can be devastating, leading to long-term emotional and mental health issues. It's crucial to remember that just because the scars aren't visible doesn't mean they're not there.

Social bullying

Also known as relational bullying, social bullying aims to damage someone's reputation or social standing. This could involve spreading rumours, excluding someone from a group, or humiliating someone in public. It's particularly insidious because it attacks the victim's social connections and friendships, which are so important during the teenage years. Victims may feel isolated, lonely, and mistrustful of others, making it hard for them to form healthy relationships in the future.

Emotional bullying

Emotional bullying targets a person's psyche, seeking to manipulate, isolate, or undermine their sense of self-worth. It's often intertwined with other forms of bullying and can be the most difficult to pinpoint. It can involve gaslighting (making someone doubt their reality), silent treatment, or manipulating someone's emotions for power. The effects can be profoundly damaging, leading to issues like anxiety, depression, and low self-esteem.

Cyberbullying

The digital age has brought with it a new form of harassment – cyberbullying. This involves using online platforms to intimidate, harass, or publicly embarrass someone. It can happen via social media, messaging apps, and within online games. One of the most dangerous aspects of cyberbullying is its omnipresence; victims can feel like there's no escape. It can lead to severe psychological stress, with victims feeling unsafe even in their own homes.

Indirect bullying

Indirect bullying is more subtle and can be harder to detect. It involves actions that aren't directly confrontational but are designed to hurt someone else. This could include spreading gossip, encouraging others to ostracise someone, or damaging someone's property. It's no less harmful than more overt forms of bullying and can leave victims feeling helpless and confused about who they can trust.

Workplace bullying

Unfortunately, bullying doesn't stop at the school gate – it can follow us into adulthood in the form of workplace bullying. This can involve similar tactics to those seen in schools, such as verbal, emotional, and social bullying, but within a professional environment. It may include undermining someone's work, constant criticism, exclusion, or public humiliation. Workplace bullying can lead to significant stress, anxiety, and can even impact someone's career trajectory.

Understanding the different types of bullying is the first step in combating it. It's crucial to foster environments – be it at school, online, or in the workplace – where respect, kindness, and empathy are the norm. If you're experiencing bullying, remember you're not alone, and there are people and organisations ready to support you. By working together, we can strive to create a world where bullying in any form is simply unacceptable.

Brainstorm

In small groups, can you think of any other types of bullying? Make a list of all the different types you can think of.

Prevalence of bullying

There are a wealth of statistics in relation to bullying both in the UK and overseas and you will regularly see bullying reported in the media. Research from the Department for Education looking at pupils in year 10 found that:

- 40% of young people were bullied in the last 12 months.
- 6% of all young people had experienced bullying daily. 9% between once a week and once a month.
- Most common form of bullying was name calling (including via text and email) at 26%, followed by exclusion from social groups at 18%.
- 21% of children who had experienced bullying daily had truanted in the last 12 months - 3 times the proportion of those who were not bullied. Young people who had experienced bullying daily also most likely to truant for the longest period of time. Girls almost twice a likely to truant because of bullying than boys.
- 24% of children bullied most days also most likely to be kept off school by their parents.
- 15% of children who had experienced bullying daily had been excluded from school in the last 12 months (compared to 5% of children not bullied).
- One in four young people with SEN (special educational needs) experienced violence (actual or threatened).
- Actual violence was more likely to always take place at school compared to other forms of bullying.

Findings from the pupil bullying and wellbeing questionnaires as part of the Anti-Bullying Alliance's United Against Bullying programme with almost 65,000 pupils across England found that:

- Almost one in four pupils reported they were bullied a lot or always.
- Pupils in receipt of Free School Meals (FSM) (28%) and those with special educational needs or disabilities (SEND) (29%) are significantly more likely to be frequently bullied.
- 6% of pupils report frequently bullying others.
- 5% of pupils report frequently being bullied online.
- Pupils who report being bullied, either face to face or online, have poorer experiences at school than those not being bullied.
- Pupils who report bullying others, either face to face or online, are the most likely to report poor experiences at school.
- Disabled children and those with SEN were around twice as likely to be bullied.
- The risk of being frequently bullied declined with age.
- Males were more likely to be victimised than females.
- Disabled children and those with SEN were three times more likely to both be bullied and bully others ('bully-victims').
- Pupils at secondary schools are significantly more likely to report having poor school experiences than primary, infant and other schools.
- Both pupils that are bullied and those that report bullying others are significantly more likely to report that they don't feel they belong at school, they don't get on with their teachers, they don't feel safe at school and they don't like going to school.
- Pupils who have been bullied and those who bully others (both face to face and online) are significantly more likely to report poor wellbeing – with those who bully the most likely to report poor wellbeing.
- Pupils at secondary school have the poorest wellbeing compared to those at primary, infant and other schools.

The above information is reprinted with kind permission from the Anti-Bullying Alliance.
© National Children's Bureau 2024

www.anti-bullyingalliance.org.uk

The majority of Britons have been bullied – and it had a significant impact on most

Schools and workplaces are at the centre of most of Britain's bullying.

By Joanna Morris

Two thirds of Britons (66%) say they have been bullied at some point in their lives, according to a new YouGov poll.

One in five people (21%) say they experienced bullying as an adult, while six in ten Britons (59%) were bullied as a child (some respondents will have been bullied in both childhood and adulthood).

Older Britons aged 65 and over are least likely to say (or remember) that they've been bullied, with 52% saying they have been, compared to between 63% and 72% of other age groups.

Those who experienced bullying as a child are most likely to say it happened repeatedly: 42% say it happened many times while a further 38% say it happened on several occasions. Only 17% say it only happened once or twice.

Bullying as an adult seems to have been less sustained: a lower figure of 23% of victims say it happened many times. Around half say they were subjected to bullying several times (47%), while 28% say it happened only once or twice.

Majority of bullied Britons say being targeted by bullies had a significant impact on their life

Three-quarters of people who were bullied as an adult say the experience impacted their life a great deal (35%) or a fair amount (39%).

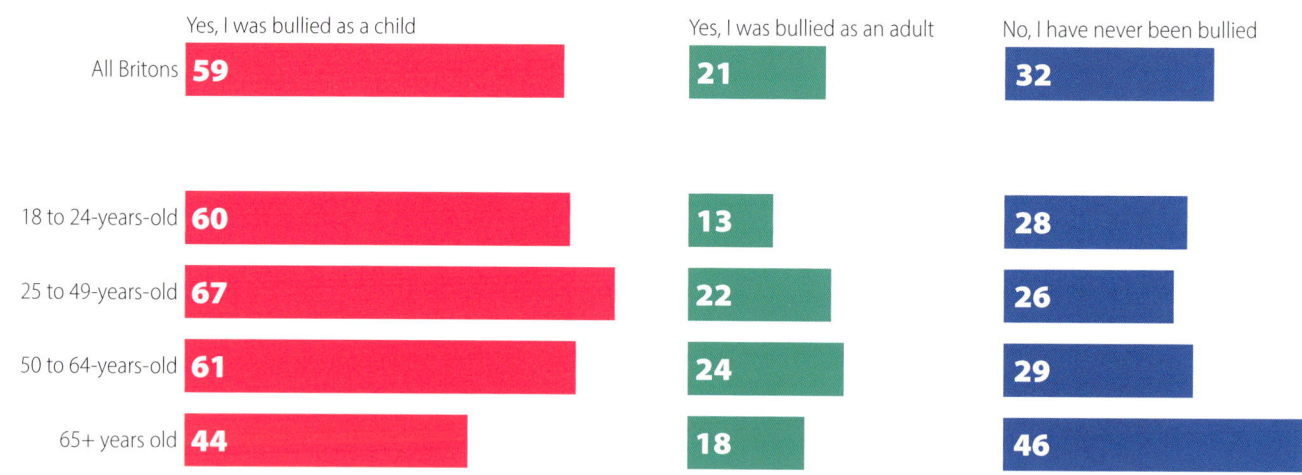

Six in ten Britons were bullied as a child - and one in five as an adult
Have you ever been bullied? Please select all that apply. %

Source: YouGov

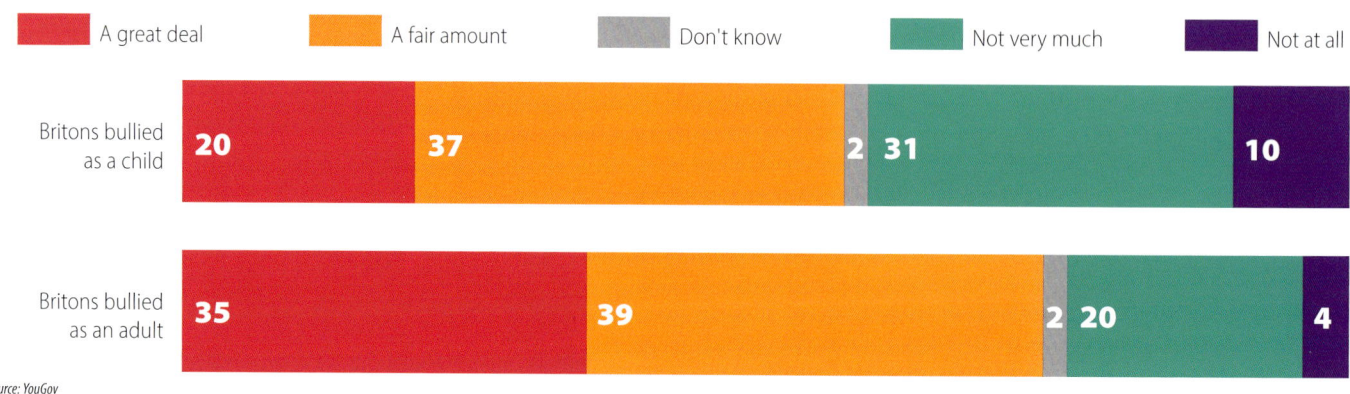

Most bullied Britons say their experiences had a great deal or fair amount of impact upon their lives
To what extent, if at all, do you think the bullying you experienced as a child/adult impacted your life?
% of 941 Britons who say they were bullied as a child and 320 Britons who say they were bullied as an adult

Source: YouGov

issues: Anti-Bullying   Chapter 1: About Bullying

In comparison, one in five of those bullied as children (20%) say it had a great deal of impact while 37% say it had a fair amount of impact on their life.

Just 4% of Britons targeted by bullies in adulthood say it had no impact on their life, while one in ten (10%) of those bullied as children say the same.

Classmates blamed by most of those bullied as children

Nearly nine in ten (87%) of those who were bullied in childhood say they were bullied by a classmate, with friends (15%) and teachers (13%) also among the culprits cited.

And a significant proportion of those Britons say they were targeted by members of their own family, including 12% who were bullied by a parent, 11% by a sibling and 5% by another family member.

Around nine in ten Britons bullied in childhood say they were targeted by their classmates

You said you were bullied as a child. Who were you bullied by? Select all that apply.
% of 941 Britons who say they were bullied as a child

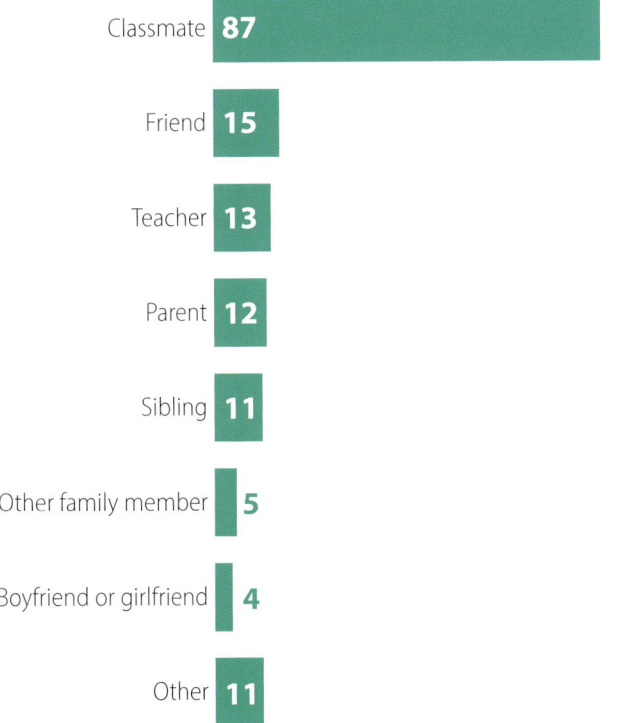

Source: YouGov

One in five bullied adults say they were targeted by their partner

A significant proportion of Britons bullied as an adult say they have suffered at the hands of those who arguably should love them the most – their spouse or partner.

One in five (20%) report being bullied by a partner, while 16% have been bullied by other family members, including 8% who say they were bullied by a parent and 6% who were bullied by a sibling.

One in five bullied adults were targeted by their spouse or partner — but the most common source of adulthood bullying is the workplace

You said you were bullied as an adult. Who were you bullied by? Select all that apply.
% of 320 Britons who say they were bullied as an adult

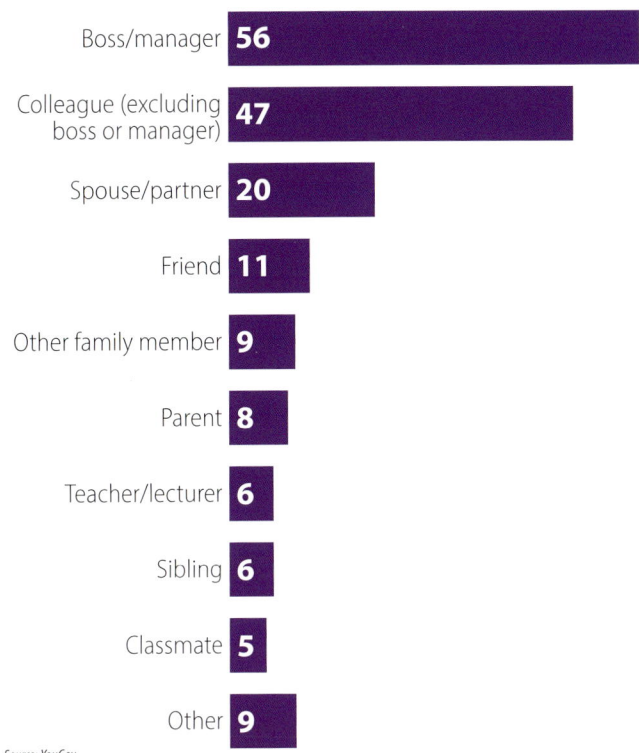

Source: YouGov

However, the most likely source of bullying in adulthood is the workplace – more than half of those bullied as adults (56%) say they have been bullied by a boss or manager and 47% by a colleague.

Most Britons bullied as children were physically attacked

Around six in ten Britons (58%) bullied in childhood say their bully physically attacked them, including 11% who say they were attacked 'many times'.

Men are more likely than women to have been physically set upon by their childhood bully, at 68% to 48%.

But when it comes to bullying in adulthood, the gender gap narrows – 21% of those who say they were bullied as an adult report being attacked at least once or twice, including 19% of men and 23% of women.

Those who were bullied in adulthood are more likely to describe the worst bullying they were subjected to as severe, with 71% of bullied adults saying it was compared to 49% of Britons bullied in childhood.

Internet brings shift in the nature of bullying for young people

The nature of bullying has shifted since the advent of the internet, with 42% of 18– to 24-year-olds who were bullied as

Nearly six in ten Britons bullied in childhood were physically attacked by their bullies, as were 21% of bullied adults

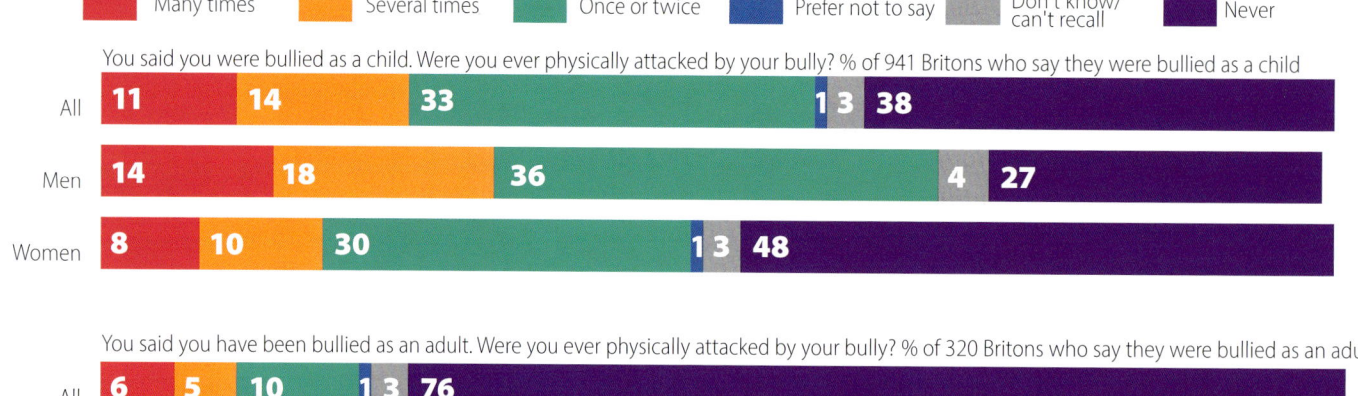

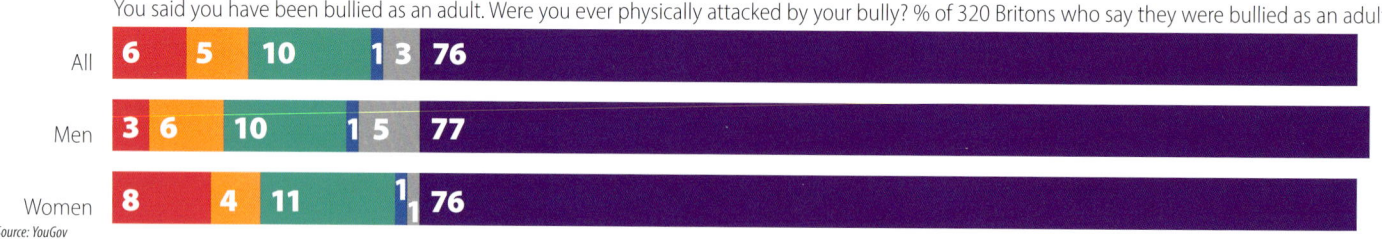

Britons bullied in adulthood more likely to describe the bullying as 'severe' than those bullied as children

For the following question, if you were bullied more than once, please think about the worst occasion. Thinking about the bullying you were subjected to as a child/adult, was it...? % of 878 Britons who say they were bullied as a child and 263 Britons who say they were bullied as an adult

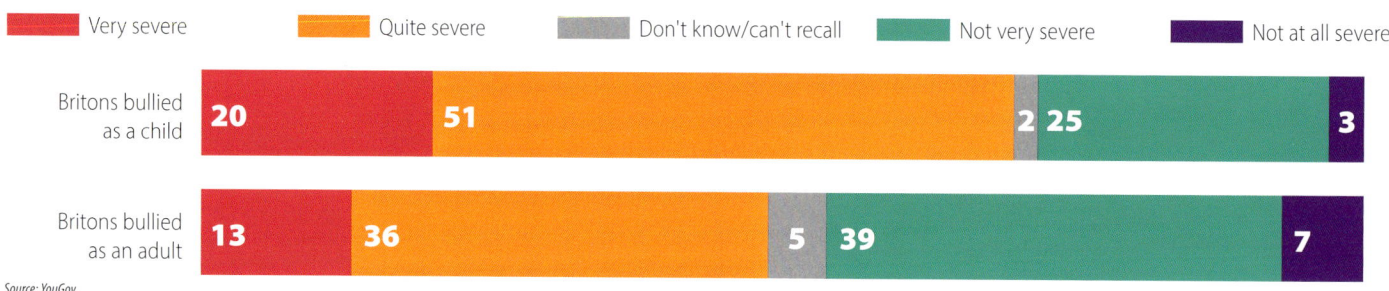

Two in five 18 to 24-year-olds who say they were bullied as a child say some of the bullying took place online

You said you were bullied as a child, did that bullying take place...
% of 941 Britons who say they were bullied as a child and 320 who say they were bullied as an adult

a child saying at least some of the bullying they experienced took place online – although almost all say they were also bullied in person.

One in six Britons (18%) who have experienced bullying as an adult say at least part of it happened online.

23 February 2023

The above information is reprinted with kind permission from YouGov.

© 2024 YouGov PLC

www.yougov.co.uk

Bullying and online experiences among children

An extract.

The 10- to 15-year-olds' Crime Survey for England and Wales (CSEW) also collects data on bullying. There is no legal definition of bullying, but it is often described as behaviour that hurts someone else, physically or emotionally, and can happen anywhere – at school, at home or online.

An estimated 1,544,000 children aged 10 to 15 years (34.9%) experienced an in-person bullying behaviour and 847,000 (19.1%) experienced an online bullying behaviour, in the year ending March 2023 (Figure 5). There was no significant difference compared with the year ending March 2020.

Figure 5

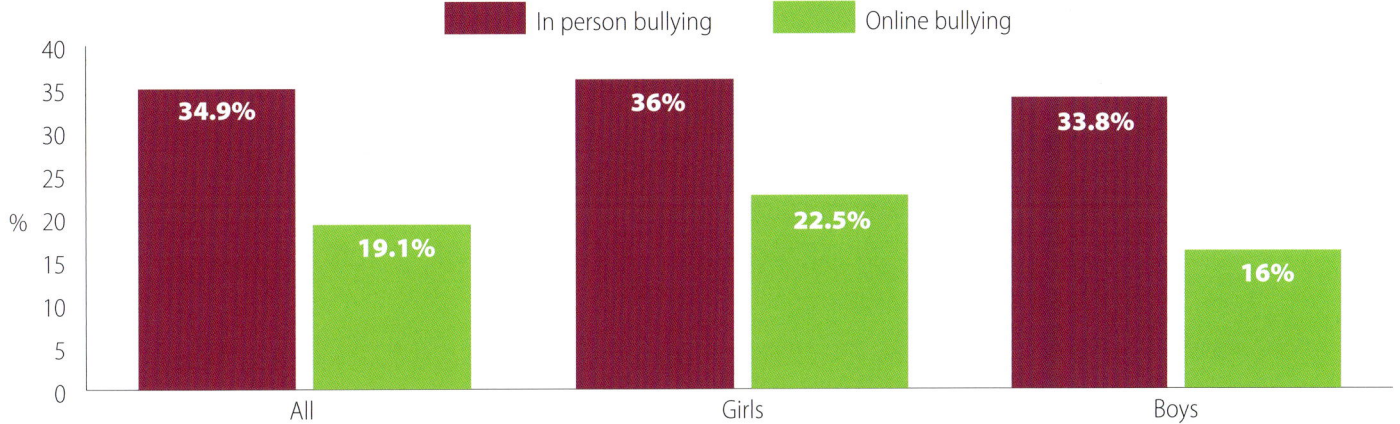

Just over a third of children experienced at least one type of in-person bullying behaviour

Proportion of children aged 10 to 15 years who experienced in-person and online bullying behaviours in the last year, by type of bullying behaviour, England and Wales, year ending March 2023

Source: 10- to 15-year-olds' Crime Survey for England and Wales (CSEW) from the Office for National Statistics

Figure 6

The most common type of in-person bullying behaviour was being called names, swore at or insulted

Proportion of children aged 10 to 15 years who experienced in-person and online bullying behaviours in the last year by type of bullying behaviour, England and Wales, year ending March 2023

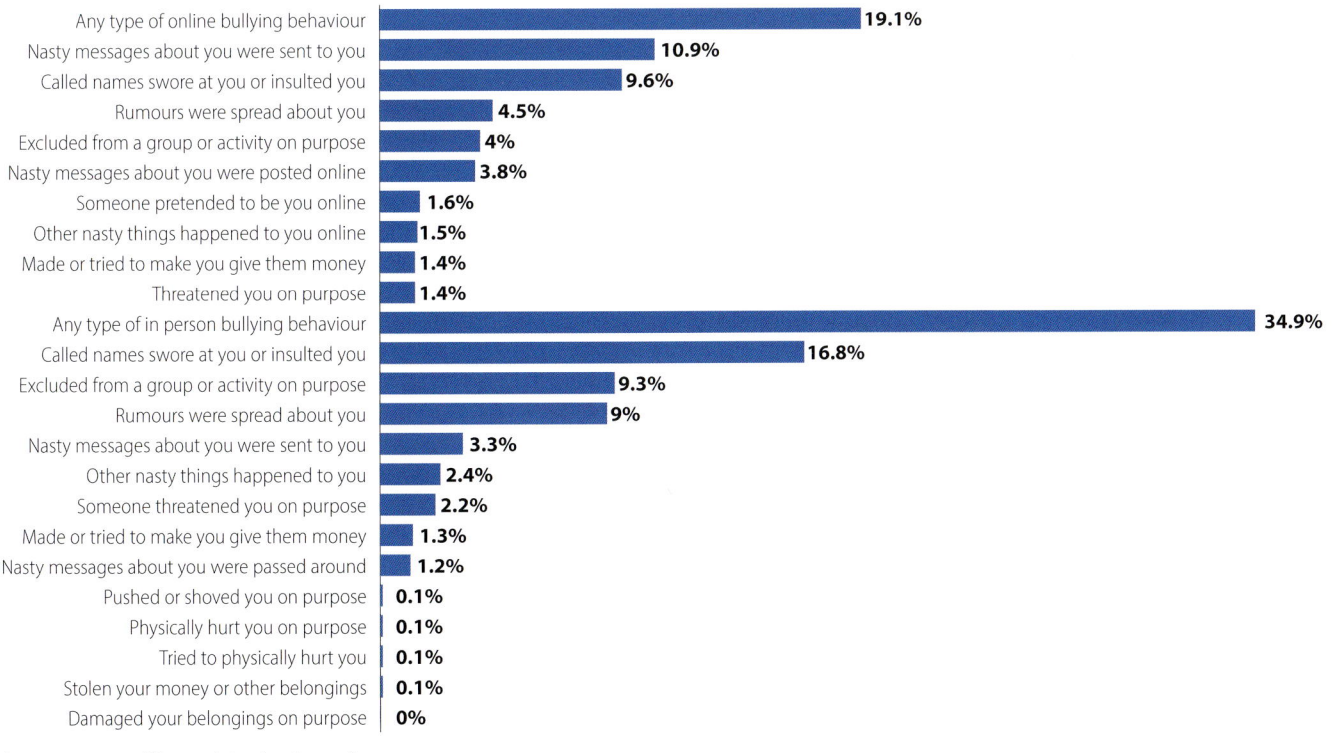

Notes: Percentages may not sum to 100 as respondents may have given more than one answer.
Source: 10- to 15-year-olds' Crime Survey for England and Wales (CSEW) from the Office for National Statistics

There was no significant difference in the estimated number of girls (779,000; 36.0%) and boys (765,000; 33.8%) who experienced in-person bullying behaviours in the year ending March 2023. However, the prevalence of experiencing online bullying behaviours was significantly higher for girls (486,000; 22.5%) than boys (361,000; 16.0%).

The most common type of in-person bullying behaviour experienced by children was being called names, swore at or insulted (16.8%), followed by being left out and excluded from a group or activity on purpose (9.3%). For children who experienced an online bullying behaviour, just over one in ten (10.9%) had received a nasty message about themselves and 9.6% had been called names, swore at or insulted (Figure 6).

Bullying can be perceived differently by individuals and can depend on the context in which something is taking place and who it is carried out by. A third (33.4%) of children who experienced in-person bullying behaviours in the last year said they would describe these behaviours as bullying compared with 45.0% of children who experienced online bullying behaviours.

Figure 7 **Most children who experienced an online or in-person bullying behaviour in the last year experienced at least some or all of it at school or during school time**

Proportion of children experiencing online and in-person bullying behaviours at school or during school time, England and Wales, year ending March 2023

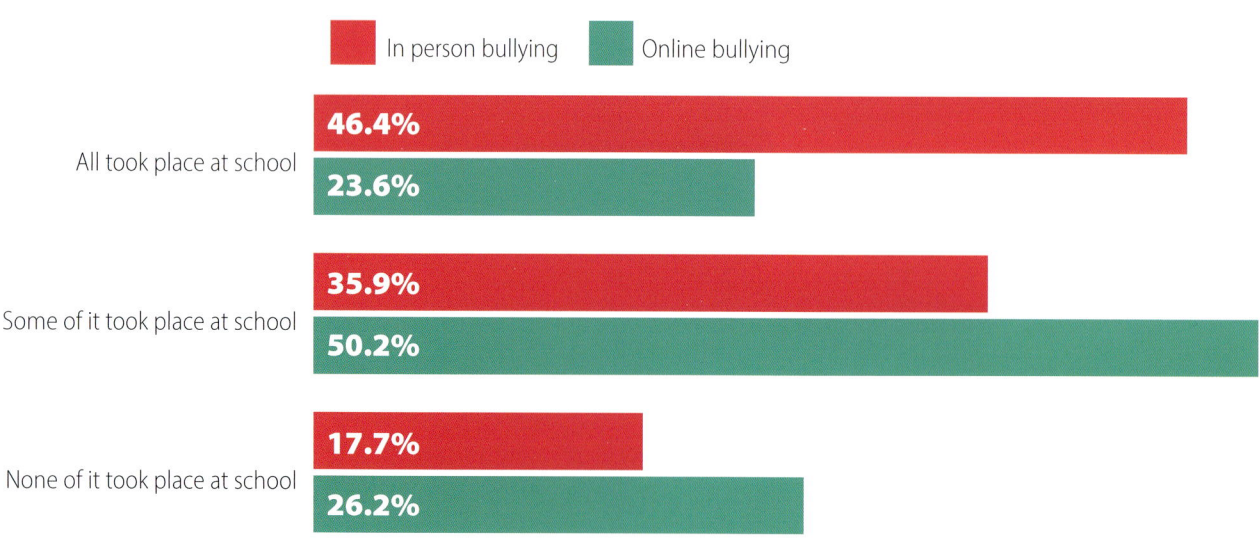

- In person bullying
- Online bullying

All took place at school: 46.4% / 23.6%
Some of it took place at school: 35.9% / 50.2%
None of it took place at school: 17.7% / 26.2%

Source: 10- to 15-year-olds' Crime Survey for England and Wales (CSEW) from the Office for National Statistics

Nature of bullying

Of all children who had experienced an in-person bullying behaviour in the last year, two-thirds (66.2%) said they had experienced two or more types of bullying behaviour. This was higher than for online bullying, with half (50.2%) stating they had experienced two or more types of online bullying behaviour in the last year.

Children were asked whether the bullying behaviours they experienced were carried out by the same person or same group of people. A similar proportion of bullying experiences were carried out by the same people, with 46.2% of children saying yes for in-person bullying and 47.4% for online bullying.

In the year ending March 2023, 67.5% of children who experienced an in-person bullying behaviour and 64.7% who experienced an online bullying behaviour said this was by someone from their school.

Children who had experienced an in-person bullying behaviour by someone at their school were more likely to say that all the bullying took place at school or during school time (46.4%) compared with children that had experienced an online bullying behaviour during school time (23.6%; Figure 7).

Bullying can have an impact on a child's emotional wellbeing. For the year ending March 2023, 18.3% of children aged 10 to 15 years who had experienced an in-person bullying behaviour and 22.7% of children who had experienced an online bullying behaviour said they were emotionally affected 'a lot' by these incidents.

Another important finding concerning schools is children's perception of how well their school deals with bullying. Most children believed that their school deals with bullying 'very well' or 'quite well'. These figures varied depending on whether children experienced at least one bullying behaviour in the last year.

For children who had experienced an in-person bullying behaviour, the percentage saying that their school deals with bullying 'not very well' or 'not well at all' was more than double (46.9%) than for children who had not (20.4%). This was similar for online bullying, with 52.9% of children who had experienced an online bullying behaviour saying that their school deals with bullying 'not very well' or 'not well at all' compared with 24.3% for children who had not experienced an online bullying behaviour.

Over half of children told their parent or guardian about the bullying they experienced in the last year (58.8% for children who experienced an in-person bullying behaviour and 56.3% for children who experienced an online bullying behaviour,) however, 18.1% who experienced an online bullying behaviour and 14.7% who experienced an in-person bullying behaviour did not tell anyone.

7 March 2024

Research

Create a questionnaire to find out if people have been bullied. Try to ask a wide range of ages and genders. What sort of bullying did they experience? Do they think that schools deal with bullying effectively?

Write

Write a letter to your headteacher explaining what you think can be done to reduce bullying in your school. Think of at least three different things that can be done to help reduce and/or prevent bullying behaviour.

The above information is reprinted with kind permission from the Office for National Statistics.

© Crown Copyright 2024

This information is licensed under the Open Government Licence v3.0
To view this licence, visit http://www.nationalarchives.gov.uk/doc/open-government-licence/

www.ons.gov.uk

Six reasons people become bullies

By Tom Turner

There appear to me to be a lot of myths surrounding the question as to why people bully. I was bullied for around eight years – probably longer. Since then I have worked with or alongside young people for 14 years, and I have worked with children for a lot longer than that. I remember one time when I had an interview for a youth work post with someone who was aware of my history of being bullied. They asked me in a very matter-of-fact way 'So, how will you stop yourself from bullying our young people?' I was quite frankly gobsmacked and astounded, but I answered her question quite clearly 'Some people who are bullied do end up bullying, but that is not a hard-and-fast rule. For me, I want to help those like me and like those who harmed me.' People get very fixated on the fact that bullies were often bullied themselves. Just as it is true that not all targets of bullying end up bullying others, it is also true that not all bullies are doing so because they were once bullied. To think this can actually be damaging to both the targets of bullying and the bully because it risks overlooking other factors that might contribute to such behaviour. Left unchecked these factors could lead to worse behaviour later on in life.

What underpins the reasons why people bully

I will look into the specifics in a minute, but I think it is vital that we understand what underpins most if not all of the reasons people bully. Most bullies have issues with power, they feel powerless in one situation and so try and find it in another. They believe they cannot take that power back from the source of the lack of power, and so deflect it onto someone they perceive as weaker than themselves. They often do this by finding the one thing that makes a person stand out from the crowd and picking on that thing. It is far easier than finding something that is hidden beneath the surface, and anyway if they did that they would probably find they liked that person and not want to bully them. I would say that most of us have unintentionally bullied someone at some point. However, what we are looking at here are the 14% who admit having deliberately bullied someone. I believe the true percentage of people to have deliberately bullied to be much higher as you have those who won't admit to it because of shame, or who see nothing wrong with what they did still.

1. Having a history of being the target of bullies

After what I've just said, I thought I better address this one first. Yes, you are more likely to bully if you have been bullied yourself. In fact, research shows that those who have been bullied are twice as likely to bully others as those who haven't. This can be a bit confusing for some people. When someone knows what it is like to be on the receiving end of bullying how could they inflict that pain on others. This view, however, discounts the effects bullying can have on someone's mental health. If you have been bullied for a significant period of time, you are going to become depressed and self-loathing. What can self-loathing do? Make you feel powerless. You are divided into two halves, the half that blames yourself for everything that has happened to you, and the other half which will want to prove that you are not that person. It is my belief that no matter how self-loathing you get, there is always a part of you that doesn't believe it, and demands proof of the contrary. One way of getting that proof is by demonstrating that someone is more loathsome than yourself, and a way of doing that is by pulling someone down lower than you.

I believe that another factor that leads to targets of bullying becoming bullies is, firstly how old they were when the bullying started, but also how much affection they got from their friends before and after the bullying. If a person has very little experience – or no memory of being treated with affection by friends then they will effectively have been programmed to think that hostility is the only way you treat people of their own age.

2. Power shifts within the family

As we know becoming a bully is an outlet for the feeling of powerlessness elsewhere. It may be unsurprising then that

children and young people who have a power shift within their family unit have an increased chance of becoming a bully within a five-year period of that power shift. When we talk about power shifts, we are of course talking about the removal of a parent from the family unit – whether through divorce or death – but also the addition of a new parent or sibling – whether step-siblings or natural ones.

These experiences can be very stressful and traumatic on people, and everybody has different ways to relieve stress. Some find a quiet place to focus on themselves and find peace, while others might express that stress violence, substance abuse and, of course, bullying.

3. They have issues at home

A third of all people who bully on a daily basis say that they have troubles at home. Often when we think about troubles at home we picture feuding or separating parents, but this is just part of the picture. When I talk about troubled homes, I am also talking about large homes where the person bullying may find it difficult to find their place being heard. Or they have issues with their step-families and have so far failed to find their place. They have strained relationships with their parents – and this could be for many reasons. Essentially they have struggled, or are struggling to find affection and affirmation from those who they need it from the most. This, of course, includes those children and young people who come from homes where violence is considered the norm.

It is interesting to note here that during my own time being bullied, about a third or more that bullied me regularly came from within the foster system; now granted, this was partly due to the fact that the taxi that served as my ride home also ferried in the students who came from a local foster home. Having seen the kinds of homes they did come from, I also wonder whether this was also a contributory factor.

4. Having insecure or manipulative friendships of their own

Making friends is an art form, but it also something we more often than not have to do on instinct alone. This is especially true when we are young as we are still learning the art form. Therefore we can easily fall into insecure or manipulative friendships. When we are in these types of friendships we can often find ourselves doing things we may not do naturally. There can be a lot of pressure to act out against someone, even if we know it is the wrong thing to do. How often do we hear about someone being bullied by a person they were friends with as a child? This often happens because they have fallen in with another group of friends who insist that they disown the old friend, for whatever reason. Then they are goaded into proving they have disowned the old friend, which results in them bullying them.

This is often done as a safety mechanism as well as fulfilling a need to fit in. Someone may bully someone else to prove they are not weak. For if they are shown to be weak in the eyes of the new friendship group they could very well become a target of bullying themselves.

5. Masculinity within our culture

Two-thirds of bullies are male. If we look at how men and women are brought up and represented in our culture then it could be very easy to see why this could be. Pretty much from the time men are born, they are told that the expression of emotion is a feminine thing and should be shied away from. We have expressions like 'Man Up', 'Take it like a man' or 'don't be a girl.'

But emotions have to be expressed somehow. If it is not done through healthy expression, then it is expressed in aggression, rage and violence. This is also the reason why boys are more likely to act out with aggression and violent self-harming. They are not necessarily born that way, it is not a case of sticks and stone etc. In reality, our society and culture have taught them that.

A good film to watch on this very subject is *The Mask You Live In* and I thoroughly encourage you to seek it out.

6. They have issues with who they are

Teenagers don't really know who they are yet. They are still seeking and searching. There can be many identity issues that a teenager could face. The most prominent ones around at the moment are those surrounding sexuality and gender. However, there are also identity issues of interests, career paths – so many we would be here forever listing them!

The issue of bullying arises here when there is someone else who perhaps is dealing with similar issues but in a more confident manner. I know that one of the reasons I was bullied was because of my physical disability. One of the main people to focus on this area as a target was someone who had recently had a lot of hospital visits themselves around that time. Though they were totally different scenarios, he saw my perceived confidence in living day to day life as an indictment on his coping with his.

The other one that always comes up from my experiences is the fact I was bullied as many people wrongly presumed I was gay. It is interesting to look back now and see how many of the boys who bullied me for this misconception are now living as gay men themselves.

To conclude

Of course, if any of these are present in the life of a child you know, it does not mean they are going to go out and bully someone tomorrow. Many people who have these in their lives live life without harming anyone else – some may even actively help others. But they are definitely at a higher risk of becoming bullies, so it is wise to keep a quiet eye, remembering two things, bullies are not evil and you know the children in your life better than I do.

The above information is reprinted with kind permission from Strength Restored.
© 2024 Strength Restored

www.strengthrestored.co.uk

Chapter 2

Effects of Bullying

How bullying harms the brain

Research pinpoints the brain-damaging force of bullying.

By Jennifer Fraser Ph.D.

> **Key points**
> - Bullying is seen as a moral issue, but a meta-analysis of research shows it's a medical issue.
> - Bullying, along with child maltreatment, can do physical damage to important brain regions.
> - The physical harm bullying does to the brain shows up in poor academic performance and mental illness.

Two researchers have found that bullying damages a number of brain regions in children. The damage is such that victims fail to understand social cues, fail to think clearly, and fail to have a handle on their own behaviour and emotions. It's devastating.

Researchers Iryna Palamarchuk and Tracy Vaillancourt conducted a meta-analysis of studies, including their own studies, on the impact of bullying victimisation on the developing brains of children. Although they focused on the amygdala, fusiform gyrus, insula, striatum, and prefrontal cortex, they acknowledge that the negative effects of bullying are not limited to such areas of the brain. They explain that neurological interplay between the regions 'contributes to the sensitivity toward facial expressions, poor cognitive reasoning, and distress that affect behavioural modulation and emotion regulation.'

In other words, when damage occurs to these brain regions, the victim may misinterpret or overreact to someone's facial expressions. While a person may show surprise, the victim's brain, harmed by bullying, may read the facial expression as angry or threatening. The brain regions malfunction, in a sense, because of bullying.

Victims may also struggle to use their rational mind to problem-solve or make decisions. Their cognition, the ability to think through challenges and problems, is impaired by bullying. Furthermore, their distressed brain may struggle to self-regulate or modulate their conduct. Likewise, their bullied brain may struggle to manage emotional outbursts or withdrawals.

What makes these injuries to the brain even more distressing is that they are invisible to the naked eye and thus most in society do not even know they have occurred. Victims know they are struggling, but few would be informed that it's because a series of regions in their brain have been harmed. Most concerning: if we do not know the brain is hurt, we do not set in motion the care needed for the brain to repair and recover. This is tragic because in fact the brain is innately wired to heal with evidence-based interventions.

How do children react who are victimised by bullying?

One manifestation discussed by Palamarchuk and Vaillancourt focuses on the way in which brain responses that naturally protect the target are thrown out of whack by the repeat nature of most bullying. Withdrawal, for instance, is an effective way the brain responds to threat out in the world, but if bullying behaviour happens repeatedly, this normally healthy brain response tilts into unhealthy territory.

The way bullying harms brain regions can lead to 'the development of mental health problems including anxiety, depression, psychosis, psychosomatic and eating disorders among bullied children.' Some children may develop emotional numbing, associated with further harm to the brain, seen in post-traumatic-stress disorder (PTSD).

It is well-established and frequently discussed in educational and parental circles that children targeted by bullying often see a drop in their grades. What is missing, however, is the brain science that informs us that poor academic performance is likely a result of 'neurophysiological changes like the ones found in maltreated children.'

What kind of physical brain changes do researchers document in maltreated and bullied brains?

Children who are abused by adults or bullied by peers may show signs of 'suppressed neurogenesis, stress-associated delayed myelination, as well as distorted apoptosis.' Scientists know that our brains produce new cells throughout our lifespan. When a brain is being abused or bullied, brain-imaging reveals, the birth of new brain cells, or neurogenesis, is compromised and in some cases halted.

Scientists know that myelination is the way the brain creates efficient, rapid, superhighways of information transmission in the brain. Myelin is a fatty insulator that wraps around axons and allows the brain to wire-in skills and knowledge through repeated practice and dedication to achievement. Children who are being maltreated or bullied suffer from delays in the critical process of laying down the myelin that helps people capitalise on their talents.

Moreover, among the bullied and abused, a normal process of apoptosis, or cell death, is 'elevated.' The cycle of cell birth and cell death is put into a state of imbalance. The target's brain struggles to birth new cells while at the same time an elevated number of cells are dying. As a result, targets suffer anxiety, depression, PTSD, poor academic performance and yet rarely know that their brain is unwell and needs help.

Chances are very good that those who abuse and bully do not know that the way they act is causing damage to a child's brain.

It is time to educate everyone about the seriously harmful impact of bullying on the brain.

As Palamarchuk and Vaillancourt demonstrate in their own studies, and in the meta-analyses they undertake into extensive research being conducted internationally, child maltreatment and peer bullying harm regions of the brain in very serious and lasting ways. This knowledge needs to be shared with all adults who are in positions of trust and authority over children.

Parents, teachers, coaches, doctors, social workers, mental health professionals need to use every opportunity to help children understand that the epidemic of mental illness in youth populations could be lessened if it were widely known that all forms of child maltreatment and bullying do damage to regions in the brain. Physical bullying may visibly harm the brain, but far more insidious is emotional, psychological, social-relational, and cyberbullying, as the damage they do to the brain is unseen. Emotional neglect, ignoring, ostracising also does deadly harm, but cannot be seen.

Where the damage can be seen and documented is in brain imaging. The knowledge researchers have gained through noninvasive technology establishes that bullying can no longer be understood merely as a moral issue. It must be understood as a medical crisis as serious as catching a potentially fatal virus.

There need to be public service announcements about the devastating invisible neurological scars bullying and child maltreatment leave on the brain. The damage can be seen on brain scans. Even more important, the damage can be repaired once acknowledged and identified.

17 June 2023

The above information is reprinted with kind permission from *Psychology Today*.
© 2024 Sussex Publishers, LLC

www.psychologytoday.com

'There's a lot of places where you can't be seen': how bullying can be invisible to adults

An article from *The Conversation*.

By Ben Arnold Lohmeyer, Lecturer in Social Work (Youth), Flinders University

School bullying is a huge and distressing problem. In 2015, 43% of Australian year 8 students experienced bullying each month. A 2022 Mission Australia survey of Australians between 15 and 19 found 47% were 'extremely' or 'somewhat' concerned about bullying.

The picture is similar overseas. In 2020, the World Health Organization reported one in three students around the world aged 11–15 years suffered bullying in the preceding month.

Despite all the research about bullying, it is rare to hear directly from young people about what bullying looks like in their everyday lives. A lot of school bullying research also relies on large-scale but shallow survey techniques.

In a new research project, I spoke to 11 young people in South Australia. Over multiple interviews and focus groups, I listened to their school bullying experiences. My approach gave young people time to think about and reflect on their experiences and provide deep insights.

My research

I asked two small groups of young people to talk with each other about what bullying and violence looked like in their school, how they define bullying and violence, and what could be done about it.

One group of young people came from a private high school and the other was from an alternative education program for disengaged young people. Some of the most striking things both groups discussed were the places and times where bullying happens.

This was not necessarily where adults or teachers expect it to happen.

Bullying happens in places where adults aren't looking

Two students told stories about the secluded places in and around schools where bullying happens, as well as students' creativity about finding them. As Drew* told me:

'There's a lot of places where you can go and you can't be seen [...] we literally kind of went around looking for all the places which were just really secluded in the school [...] we found way more than we were expecting to. And then we just realised like, wow, it's a lot of places where people could just do not good stuff here.'

Similarly, Alex said bullying did not often happen in the schoolyard because 'the teachers are around'.

'But it can [happen] on social media, at say where people go to catch their buses after school and stuff, that's really common [...] after you leave the school gates. And everyone's catching buses home and stuff in places where people drink alcohol obviously, the bay and in town that's like really common.'

But it can happen out in the open

Some participants talked about spaces in schools that encourage bullying or violence. These were public places, but did not necessarily have a teacher around. Two interviewees talked about 'the spine', a long corridor through their school. As Mason said:

'There is a long hallway down the entire school [...] And because the hallway that went through the school was only about, I'd say, four people wide [...] they [bullies] would just line up and just try and bump people out of the way.'

Owen noted that students were aware of the dangers of this area.

'You see a group of kids come through the spine [...] and you'd be like, "oh what's happening?", and they'd be like, "oh someone is gonna go start a fight over here, let's go", and then it's just like, "oh ok".'

These comments show how the shape and size of spaces in schools can encourage bullying and violence. This suggests the planning and architecture of a school can make a big difference in bullying.

And it can even happen around teachers

Classrooms and schoolyards where teachers are present are expected to be safe spaces. But the young people in our research said bullying can be hidden by the expectation that young people should deal with these problems themselves, or that this behaviour is normal. As Owen explained:

'If you're a victim, it can and can't be stopped. Like you can, you can stop it but like, it's seen as [being] a pussy, if you're going to go to the teacher all the time and be like, "This kid's bullying me". But like, you know, if a c*** is just being annoying, then just go. Go to the teacher and just be like, "Nah f*** that guy, like he's being a dick", like 24-7'.

Although there did seem to be limits to students' violence or bullying around adults. This is particularly the case in classrooms or alternative school spaces with lots of teachers and extra support around. As Drew described:

'The point is, there are literally teachers around nearly everyone [...] So, if you were going to bully someone in there, you're literally a f****** idiot'.

We need a better understanding of bullying

Young people in this research talked about how bullying is hidden by physical buildings and social expectations in schools. To tackle this problem, research and policy need to move beyond interventions just focused on individuals (that is, victims, perpetrators and bystanders).

We also need to listen closely to young people's experiences of physical and social space. This could help us understand not only when and where bullying happens, but also why bullying is sometimes invisible to adults.

*Names have been changed

11 December 2022

Brainstorm

Can you think of any areas in your school where bullying is more likely to take place? What could be done to prevent bullying in these places?

THE CONVERSATION

The above information is reprinted with kind permission from The Conversation.

© 2010-2024, The Conversation Trust (UK) Limited

Suffering PTSD from school bullying: My search for validation

It took me a long time to get rid of the shame that plagued me after my experience at school, and the reason for that lies in a portion of society's refusal to recognise being bullied as a serious and traumatic experience.

[This article contains themes of abuse and accounts of personal trauma]

By Hannah Broughton

Conversations around trauma and mental health in all their complicated forms have become less taboo in the last couple of decades, and you'd have to be a hermit not to notice.

One of the most commonly experienced catalysts for trauma and mental health conditions, such as anxiety and depression, is bullying, with an estimated prevalence rate of 32% in schools and 30% in workplaces.

It's hard to know whether this estimation is at all accurate because so many children and adults don't report their experiences of bullying. Despite it being described as an 'epidemic' and on the rise worldwide, bullying is still often dismissed as just being a difficult but normal part of life.

When I was at secondary school I was bullied and physically attacked by a group of girls. After years of name-calling and general taunting, they physically attacked me after a PE lesson. The following week one of them waited outside my geography lesson with a group of older boys and did it again.

My school did little to make me feel supported when I was bullied. My teachers were more interested in reminding me that while I came from a 'good home', my attackers had chaotic lives. How dare I complain about something so trivial as bullying when I should just be grateful I have a good home life?

This, I believe, greatly contributed to my PTSD, because it added to the shame of it all. I was deeply ashamed of myself for existing and being who I was because clearly, I deserved to be treated this way.

I did everything I could to disappear. This became harder to do when, as a consequence of the bullying, I moved to another, much posher secondary school that was known for excelling in Drama, so there were loads of incredibly confident children from wealthy backgrounds – a stark difference to my previous school. I didn't adjust to it well and quickly started to feel like an outsider.

I skipped classes on my own, drank alcohol in school, did some controversial things at parties, and started going clubbing even though I was well below the legal age.

While a lot of this was fairly normal amongst my friends, I was partly doing this to self-medicate my overwhelming feelings of self-hatred and anxiety.

Just after I was attacked, a lot of people were understanding and shocked by it. As time went on, however, people had less patience. I ended up being ridiculed by a friend at my new school for never speaking, as they had grown tired of it and my silence was making things awkward for them.

A few years later I was talking to my then-boyfriend about how I was still feeling upset about what had happened to me. He was confused and told me that I didn't even get 'beat up that bad' so why was I still so affected by it?

This all happened in the noughties, just before the world woke up to the importance of mental health. Attitudes were better than say in the 70s, but, apart from professionals, nobody really understood how anxiety or PTSD worked, nor did they care much.

When I eventually went to university in 2010, I had another huge bout of anxiety and started taking medication for the frequent and terrifying panic attacks I was having. I also began going to counselling sessions that the university was offering its students for free.

It is quite spectacular just how unhelpful these sessions were. The two therapists I saw there seemed frustrated that I hadn't come to them with a juicy story they could get their teeth into, it was just a boring school bullying story.

The first therapist would try and compete with me in regards to how depressed I was, and say things like 'Well, when I was depressed I couldn't even get out of bed, and I couldn't even make myself a cup of tea.'

She seemed to sneer at my problems of panic attacks and feeling like everyone hated me. I eventually stopped seeing her and tried somebody else at the university.

This one was even worse – she would say things like 'We deal with people who have been raped, who have had awful things happen to them' and tell me I should feel happy this wasn't me.

When we had our last session I cried and told her I don't know if I can cope, and I remember her looking at me with this irritated look on her face and telling me I would be fine.

When it comes to the long-term effects of PTSD, you often feel like you're on your own, and that can be debilitating. You desperately want to be understood by others and you want to understand yourself, but it isn't straightforward.

People expect the longest forms of PTSD to be from the most horrific unthinkable things, how could anyone be so affected by something that happened to them at school? I felt guilty about my feelings for so long, I just wanted to delete them and be normal, but I couldn't.

I asked London-based therapist Gail Rhodes why some people are affected by trauma for longer periods than others.

'A person with a less sensitive nature and more secure internal base which developed from receiving solid dependable care as a small child is better able to cope with difficult life events than someone whose early experiences and attachments were less secure. It's the extent to which trauma can be digested and metabolised in the mind and body which dictates how long the trauma impacts.'

I had a very stable and loving childhood when I was a lot younger, but since starting secondary school, life had become less stable, and that was simply because my secondary school was very chaotic.

Children would roam the halls during lesson time, entering classrooms they knew had supply teachers, or less assertive teachers, and cause havoc. My friend had her hair set on fire while on one of the school buses, and our lessons were regularly interrupted by fire alarms due to arson attacks on school toilets.

School time became less about learning and more about ensuring you weren't a target for humiliation or worse. This brings me to another theory of why some are more resilient to trauma than others.

'Sometimes when we talk about trauma, we talk about a "dose-response relationship," which simply means that a person's response to trauma is directly related to the amount of exposure he or she has,' explains Dr Sunda Friedman TeBockhorst in her blog post *What Makes Some People More Resilient to Trauma Than Others?*

'Because of the differing "doses," a person who experiences a single-incident trauma of brief duration (a car accident, for example) is at less risk of lasting problems than a person who experiences chronic exposure to ongoing traumatising events for a lengthy period (such as child abuse or neglect).'

This would explain why bullying can leave such a lasting effect on its victims because the traumatic events are often sustained for a long time rather than experienced as one isolated event.

One thing I have is a sensitive nature, which is something I tried to shake off throughout my teens and twenties – probably as a response to the trauma that the bullying had caused me. I eventually realised it can't be done, and nor should a person's sensitivity be diminished. It's growing on

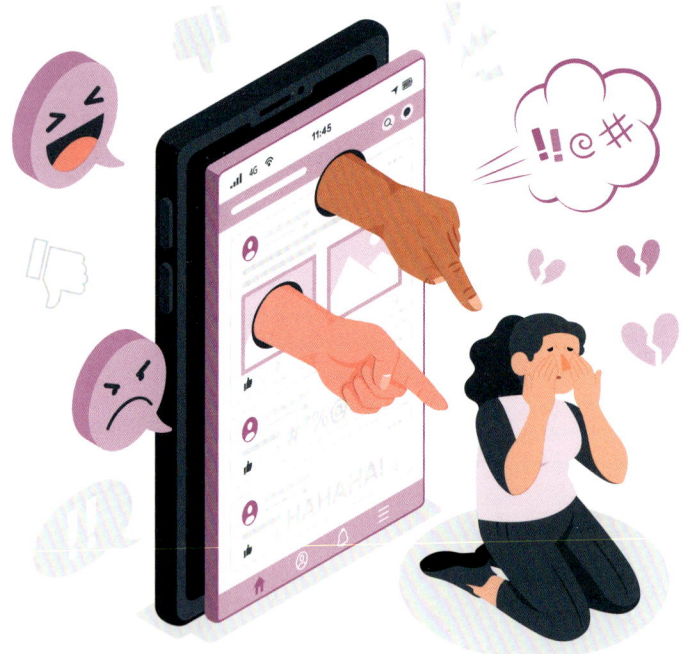

me now – I've accepted it and I accept the positives and negatives that come with it.

To think that around 32% of children are bullied at school these days, I worry for children who are enduring similar things to what I went through, especially those who don't have the support system in their family as I had. We now have the added risk of cyberbullying, which is an ever-growing concern for parents and teachers.

Since I left secondary school, not only has awareness of mental health issues changed rapidly, but technology and the internet have grown exponentially. There is an abundance of platforms built for sharing things about ourselves, and many people have taken to sharing traumatic experiences for the world to see.

I wonder what are the lines we should work within when it comes to sharing details about our trauma online? Take a look at 'TraumaTok', reported on by *Vice* last year, where individuals film themselves speaking about personal traumatic things that have happened to them – using hashtags #traumadump and #trauma.

After diving into those hashtags I challenge anyone not to feel at least a little overwhelmed. Some of the first-hand accounts of trauma from TikTokers are horrific to hear, with many detailing experiences of rape, incest, violence, and severe abuse.

I can see how it could consume vulnerable young people, and worryingly TikTok might be the only outlet some people have to feel validated and listened to. Validation, after all, is a huge part of why social media in general exists, is it not?

But, ultimately, this is about choices, and we all have a choice whether to share or not to share. 32-year-old Natalie was also bullied at school and still suffers PTSD effects from it now, and she has found comfort in TikTok posts from strangers.

'You have to be careful with what you're letting yourself listen to. It can be a bit too much sometimes. When you get people talking about being molested and raped and all sorts of things, it's very hard to listen to, but I understand that people have to speak their truth and for some people, it's very healing for them too. It's healing for them to be able to say it out loud,' she explains.

'You're able to see lots of different people, and it's not just celebrities and it's not all just filtered things. You get to see the average person talk about their experiences – good or bad, and I think that's quite interesting.

'I've learned more about my mental health and my traumatic experiences, and I've learned more about that through people sharing their experiences. And you know, as much as we like to think we're very individual, and we are obviously, but we have lots of shared experiences.'

'I've managed to get through some really dark times, like break-ups, and all sorts of things, by the empowerment of strangers on the Internet – it gives me different perspectives on how to think about things, and different points of views, and different ways to move forward.'

Does she think it would have helped her when she was younger, and going through issues at school?

'I feel like for me it probably would have. I almost wish I was able to understand all these things a hell of a long time ago because I feel like I wouldn't have stuck around for a lot of things that I did stick around for.'

I am sceptical of whether or not TraumaTok is for me, but I can empathise with why Natalie finds it helpful. I decided to search for clips specifically talking about bullying and trauma, to see what that brings up.

After scrolling through for about 20 minutes, I start to realise that things might not have changed as much as I thought they had since I was at school. Not only is this still something many children and teenagers are tackling, but there are videos implying that victims feel let down by their schools and this one coincides with my theory that many still don't take bullying seriously.

TikTok is clearly a goldmine of useful information for young people, but I see a lot of pitfalls in problematic ways of thinking there as well.

One of the things I struggled with a lot whilst coming to terms with what happened to me and how it affected me, is the shame of it all. I ask therapist Gail Rhodes what her advice is to those struggling with feelings of shame and guilt around their response to trauma.

'When a person is struggling with shame due to experiences that were inflicted on them – i.e., not their own actions – I sometimes ask them to imagine a dear friend or family member, someone they care for deeply, and imagine that person describing having experienced what the person in question has experienced,' Gail explains.

'I ask them to imagine this person describing being bullied in the same way, how frightening it was, how it affects them deeply to this day and then to imagine them saying they feel ashamed of this having happened, guilty, embarrassed, etc.

'I then ask what they would say to that person, and if they think that this person should be feeling embarrassed because they're struggling with these matters,' Gail said.

Invariably the answer comes back as 'No, of course not, they have nothing to feel embarrassed about', so Gail asks them what they imagine their friend might need from them, and usually receives answers such as love, a hug, kindness, and being listened to.

'I then ask that they consider the idea that that is what they need to try to direct towards themselves, the same compassionate, loving kindness that they would offer a loved one – instead of blaming themselves for what happened, for how it is affecting them now, and therefore perpetuating the cycle of shame,' Gail continues.

I eventually found solace in a good therapist and the right medication, and while I will probably always grapple with issues that were born out of a difficult time in my life, those issues get smaller each time I successfully ignore them.

My guilt and shame around what happened to me are rooted in how others responded to my pain in the past, but ultimately I should never have relied on the validation of others when it came to my personal experience.

This is perhaps a process everyone has to go through when they experience something that causes them initial feelings of shame, but the day that you truly realise you don't have to live by others' judgements of you, is the day you start to feel a lot lighter.

Whichever way each individual chooses to get to that point, it should be celebrated.

8 June 2023

Write

Write down some ideas for things that you think may help someone deal with trauma from bullying.

Consider...

Do you think that turning to social media for support is a good thing? Or, do you think that it is potentially dangerous, as it may lead to someone finding distressing or harmful content?

Where would you go to to find support? Can you think of a reliable source of support?

The above information is reprinted with kind permission from *Artefact Magazine*.
© Artefact magazine / LCC / UAL – 2014-24
www.artefactmagazine.com

Could you forgive your childhood bully? Katy Wix confronts a painful memory

When the actor and comedian's teenage best friend suddenly became her cruel tormentor, Katy Wix's mum told her to be patient and not to let it get to her. But it did. Decades later, a message arrives out of the blue…

By Katy Wix

In the same way that when you are full you can't imagine being hungry, when you have a best friend you can't imagine being their enemy.

I was in bed. I had bought a 2m-long phone charger so I could comfortably play Cake Shop 2 while lying down when, bored of my own peace, I went on Instagram. Among the usual DMs – one from a non-profit sunglasses company saying, 'We love your account's vibe', a man saying, 'My dog has drawn you', and an invite to be on a podcast about DJing – was the message from her.

I zoomed in on her profile picture. It was my best friend from secondary school. The same teenage features, now stretched into an adult's face, were sitting in a car holding a Chilly's water bottle, with a smile the same shape as if she were midway through brushing her teeth. The name I've chosen to pretend her name is, is 'Erin'. I didn't open the message.

I met her one summer evening by the stone wall that always had teenagers puking or falling over near it. She was smoking, in the dark, with two other girls from the village, their cigarettes glowing like the electric bars on my nan's old heater. When she clicked her lighter, the flame made her eyes look huge, like moons. But up close I could see this was just the effect of layers of black liquid eyeliner. I said I liked her jacket while looking at my shoes. She said, 'Thanks' and called some boys over. Without discussion, we became best friends.

We spent all summer in her baby-pink bedroom making up dances, taking it in turns to say what we thought a 'blowjob' was and placing phone books on our lower stomachs to imagine what the weight of another person would feel like there. I knew we would speak every day for the rest of our lives.

So why was she messaging me now, years later? I chewed off a cuticle and opened the message. But instead of reading it, I held the message away from my face like it might go off, and imagined what it said. Maybe she had good news. Maybe she had bad news. Maybe someone had died. Maybe she had died and this was her child or mum hopping on to her account to tell me. Maybe the recent 90s fashion renaissance had triggered in her a wave of nostalgia. I remembered one of her short stories winning a prize at our school eisteddfod: maybe she wanted writing advice. Maybe she wanted help getting verified. Maybe it's a bot. Maybe she's selling a table.

My phone screen locked and went black. In the screen's reflection, an adult was staring back at me. For a moment, I forgot I wasn't 14.

One lunchtime, Erin pointed at a tall boy with red cheeks and said, 'That's Owain. He's the one I fancy.' Later, Owain came up to me in the library and said, 'Do you want to get off with me after school?' But Erin liked him and I hadn't kissed anyone yet and didn't know the tongue movements, so I said no. That afternoon, I was in an art lesson, copying an ankh from a book on Egyptian art, when everything changed.

Erin was silent. 'Your ankh's really realistic,' I said. But she didn't reply. Instead she got up and, with her half-finished drawing, went and sat on the table behind me. Then, she gestured to the other girls to join her. As stools scraped, I sat confused at the centre of a flurry of charcoals and A3 heavyweight paper, and was left on my own. I was stunned by Erin enforcing this strange new power, like the first time I saw an adult put out a candle with their fingers.

Maybe it was a joke I didn't get. So I just giggled and carried on drawing the ankh. But then I felt Erin point at me and say to her table: 'Is she wearing shoulder pads? Why are her shoulders so wide?' Everyone laughed. I didn't turn round and hoped she'd think I was too engrossed in cross-hatching my ankh to hear her. I swung my legs on the stool with such performative nonchalance that, if the Big Brother body language expert had seen me, she would have said: 'This girl is fine.' Then Erin kicked my stool and I turned to her as if I'd forgotten she was there and she said, 'Why would Owain like you? Look at your fringe. Who cut it: a bimbo?'

I rested my head in my hand, pressing my hair into my ear, but their laughter and voices still came through the hair barrier. I couldn't hear the words, but I could feel them in my stomach, like a distant drum beat. I felt my face go red like someone had got the trainer bra and pants from my bedroom and was holding them up, one by one, on the six o'clock news. At the end of the lesson, the teacher looked at my ankh and said that one side was very realistic, but the other side was sloppy.

That night, I couldn't focus on my homework. I looked out of my bedroom window at every noise that sounded like her bike, thinking she was coming over to say sorry. But she didn't.

I told my mum what happened. Without stopping moisturising her neck, she said: 'You'll be friends again tomorrow.' I didn't move. So she turned around, put two creamy hands on my shoulders, smiled lovingly, and said: 'Don't let it get to you.'

Whenever I spoke in class, Erin would do an impression of my lisp and whisper, 'Who's that stupid toddler?' But I didn't let it get to me. When she said to me in the girls' changing room, 'I wouldn't wear sleeveless tops if I were you,' the shame made me nauseous, but I didn't let it get to me. When she said on the bus, 'Why is your hair so greasy – can't you afford shampoo?' my hands tingled with hurt, but I didn't let it get to me. I grew out my fringe thinking that it would protect me, and I hung out with another sad girl even though I didn't like her, because it was 1% less bad than being alone. But I didn't let it get to me.

'Just be patient,' my mum said as she trimmed my fringe over the bathroom sink. 'It'll all be over soon.' At the word 'patient' I suddenly had a plan: I would just hold all the pain inside and wait for the bullying to stop. Being patient was something I was good at. When I would pick out a party dress from my mum's Next catalogue, it would take six weeks to arrive, but the waiting was easy. Because I just knew that once I owned that party dress, I would be so happy. (I still feel this way about dresses now.)

Back in my bedroom, I brought the phone closer to my face and sat up, barely scratching the surface of the slack of the 2m cable. In the old 1m days, I would have been rebounded by the stinginess of the cable, and this move would have been impossible.

I unlocked my phone to reveal the message again. It was only a few lines long. I skimmed its surface, like when you open a letter that informs you whether you have passed or failed something and you look for a word like 'delighted' or 'unfortunately'. I had a sudden urge to sleep, which always happens when I want to avoid something. My shoulders were hunched up close to my ears and my mouth was dry. I forced myself to start at the beginning of the first sentence and to read it properly.

It ended with a fight. Erin said she wanted to meet me in the local park. I didn't want to go, but the shame of not going was greater than the fear of going. And the hardest thing to have patience for is your own shame.

There was nothing in *Mizz* magazine about how to choose an effective weapon, or how to sneak it out of the house while your parents were watching Coronation Street. So I took a golf umbrella from beside the front door.

The fight began. Erin's weapon of choice was her cherry red Dr Martens with steel toe caps. She tried to kick me and I waved the end of the golf umbrella at her. As her hand came towards my face, I thought, 'There's the hand I put a friendship bracelet on, the hand that made pizzas from scratch in my kitchen with me and my mum, the hand that painted my nails.' As I tried to anticipate the arc of her hand's movement, we briefly made eye contact. Once, I would stay up all night and look into those eyes, rather than fall asleep for a second, because I wanted to keep talking. Now, those eyes were trying to hurt me.

Eventually a woman and her beagle ran over to intervene. I wondered if we'd be sent to borstal and whether I'd be allowed to ask for separate cells. Erin spat on the ground in front of me and said, 'You're not worth it anyway.' Those were the last words we exchanged.

Until now. Her message said: 'I'm sorry I was such a bitch. Can you forgive me?'

'That's so nice,' I thought. I started typing a reply: 'Hey! It's fine! It was all such a long time ago.' I thought, 'This is the right thing to do.' I continued to type: 'Of course I forgive you. I never think about it.' And I thought to myself, as women think to themselves hundreds of times a day: 'It wasn't that bad.' When I finished typing, there were red crescents in my palm where I had dug my nails into my hand. I deleted my draft reply.

How bad was it, really? I didn't wear a sleeveless top in public until I was 32, because of what she said about my shoulders, but it could have been worse: I could have been 35. I only spent a year in speech therapy to get rid of my lisp. And I've only mentioned her about once a month in therapy, definitely not every week. How do you calculate the impact another person has had on you? Well, it's either ruined my life, or it's fine.

The real shame was not that it happened or that I didn't stand up for myself. The real shame was that the advice I was given could not attend to the wild recesses of the heart of a teenage girl. So I mistook patience for strength and repression for serenity. It was the wrong solution. But I get to do it differently now.

When the bullying was most intense, I would eat lunch alone in a toilet cubicle and pretend I was an adult looking back on my life and I would be successful and I would be laughing about it. So there was pressure on me now, as the grown woman that I had imagined. The 14-year-old was waiting for me to do something.

Back in my bedroom, half-lit by the light of the phone, I thought about my mum, and her mum, and the long line of women I come from who were all experts at minimising their own pain. Even Erin must have had to minimise her own pain, in order to inflict it on another person. I wondered what she was going through back then.

But I had to do things differently. I had to let it get to me. So I replied on that 14-year-old's behalf, with the truth. 'I don't forgive you,' I typed. And pressed send.

7 July 2024

The above information is reprinted with kind permission from *The Guardian*.
© 2024 Guardian News and Media Limited

www.theguardian.com

I will never forgive my school bullies – that would only help them, not me

By Dayna McAlpine

'Oh my god Dayna, I almost didn't recognise you there!'

My heart dropped as I faced the person beaming at me, their hand gripped on my arm to stop me in my tracks.

My mouth went dry as I faced the older version of a high school memory that I'd spent years pushing out of my mind.

'I hear you're doing so well these days right? Big jumps since school, eh?'

I stared blankly as it all flashed in front of me. The bullying I suffered at the hands of this person, and of my peers.

Whispers quiet enough to bring tears to my eyes but not loud enough for the teachers to hear.

The stabbing pain of an elbow rammed into my ribs 'by accident'. The smirks, the stares, the made up rumours, the never-ending reminders that I wasn't enough.

The girls who claimed to be 'fine with me' but who threw their heads back and cackled as they saw their peers terrorise me.

The terrifying and desperate want for it all to end; feelings my teenage brain just couldn't handle.

And then I saw her in my mind: the 14-year-old version of myself, hiding in the furthest corner of our garden, sobbing into the fur of our concerned family dog, aching from isolation.

Something snapped.

'Sorry,' I said, swiping my arm away before asking, 'Who are you?' I knew exactly who they were, but I wasn't about to give them the satisfaction.

'Oh, from high school y'know, I…'

I had already started walking away.

'Yeah, sorry, I'm super busy.'

I know what you might be thinking – that's a bit petty, no? Time goes by, people grow up and it's always best to 'forgive and forget'.

But what if you don't want to? Because who is my forgiveness – given without ever seeing a hint of accountability from the perpetrators – really benefiting?

I remember being told by a school counsellor, as I finally confided the extent of my suffering and its impact, that, 'They're probably jealous of you' and, 'You never know what they have going on at home'.

Even at 14, I was baffled. Accepting either of those facts wasn't going to stop my fear of walking down the school's corridors and hearing the hissing comments fired in my direction; as if I'd forgotten I was worthless in the time it had taken them to breathe in between each one.

Instead of action being taken against their behaviour, I was being asked to pardon people who weren't looking for my absolution. How the hell was 'be the bigger person' the supposed solution?

Now, letting things go seems to be the almighty sign that, 'Yes, congratulations, you have officially moved on!' like somehow withholding it is a sign of incomplete healing.

That's just not true.

The fact is, you can move on without dishing out forgiveness to those who hurt you most.

Well into my twenties, the echoes of their comments would wrap around me as I scrutinised every bit of myself in the mirror. They'd roar in my head as I tried to make new friends at university, taunting me with the idea that I'd never be accepted or liked.

There'd be nights where I'd start to shake with panic for no reason and my anxious mind would transport me back to my teenage self, the memories swirling around my brain.

Pardoning people for causing this doesn't stop it all from having happened in the first place. Nor would it have suddenly stopped my suffering from the trauma of it all in the years that followed. My peace with being bullied to this extent was made between the four walls of an NHS therapist's office and it took a whole lot of work.

I've moved on, but I have not and will not forgive and forget.

Now – at almost 30 years old – excusing the five, miserable years of bullying I endured won't help me or add anything more of value to my 'healing journey'. I'm past it. It all still happened, but now I carry it with me in a different, healthier way.

My mind no longer reverts to a teenage version of myself whenever I'm hurt. A bad day is now just a bad day like anyone else's, not a 24-hour affair of reaffirming my insecurities with words spoken 15 years ago.

What happened to me is now my driving force, as I strive to live the life I want. My emotional scars run deep, but my determination to succeed is my own brand of Bio-oil fading them.

I feel a sense of relief as I look at my life and see a version of myself that I could only dream of in my teens. I didn't need to have a big, ethereal moment of excusing everything to suddenly feel truly free – I just, with the help of so very much therapy, moved on.

However, my self-imposed mission to hold my teen bullies to account will have zero effect on them in reality – it won't even occur to them that their damage lasted for decades after that school bell rang for the last time.

And, for the same reason, I will not let them off the hook.

Forgiveness is reserved for those who seek it – and it's not being sought by the people from my past who follow my every move on Instagram, sending heart-eye emojis to my latest articles as if they didn't laugh when I was reduced to tears.

It's not being sought when I get a message saying, 'Hey! Long time no speak! I'd love your advice on getting into the media' as if we'd ever previously spoken beyond their cruel comments and my deathly silence.

And as I felt that hand grip my arm in the street and saw the face of a person completely complicit in my suffering, it hit me.

This person had decided that I would be fine and would have moved on – and now, after years of feeling totally out of control, this was something I could take charge of.

If someone took the time to acknowledge their part in the hurt inflicted on me in my teens, I'm still not convinced I'd be able to let bygones be bygones.

If they at least took a shred of accountability, it would bring a sense of validation that yes, the pain I went through was absolutely not OK, but some things are just too big to forget altogether.

It is not anyone else's decision as to whether or not I choose to forgive them.

Being unable to excuse the people who caused me pain doesn't make me a bad person. I might not think of them every day anymore, I might not actively hate them or wish them misfortune, I might no longer dwell on why such things happened to me or wonder what my life would have been like had it not.

But I absolutely do not forgive a single person involved in the trauma inflicted on my life and I don't think anyone should be pushed to do so in theirs.

It's time to stop seeing letting go of trauma as the benchmark for 'completely healed'. And if you think I'm wrong, well, you don't have to forgive me for what I've said.

21 January 2023

Consider...

Do you think its possible to forgive and forget bullying?

The above information is reprinted with kind permission from *Metro* & DMG Media Licensing.
© 2024 Associated Newspapers Ltd

www.metro.co.uk

From friendship to fear: my journey through school bullying and its lasting impact

By Danielle Lobban

I was bullied in secondary school from Year 8 until halfway through Year 10, when my parents finally pulled me out because it was seriously affecting my physical and mental health.

Before that, I had the occasional issue on the playground, but the school handled things quickly, and they blew over. That all changed when a new girl, Claire*, joined our school. She'd been expelled from her previous school, unbeknownst to me at the time, for bullying other students, and my head of year asked me to 'buddy up' with her. We became friends, even though my other friends didn't like her. But I told them not to be mean – she was new, and I wanted to give her a chance. My parents even took her out with us for dinner, to the cinema, bowling, etc. Soon, though, my old friends stopped hanging out with me, and I found myself left with Claire and a couple of girls I wasn't really close to. I didn't realise it at the time, but that's when the bullying started. Claire made me feel isolated, spreading rumours about me and telling me that my friends were saying horrible things behind my back. And I believed her.

Eventually, others started joining in too. I understand now they were probably scared of her, so it was easier to side with her than defend me. Then the bullying got worse. I started getting nasty phone calls at home. My parents had to change our number and stop me from answering the phone. I wasn't even allowed to give my friends the new number because we had no way to block or identify callers back then. I was terrified every time the phone rang, not knowing what they would say.

One day on the bus home from school, a group of girls stuck a huge lump of chewing gum in my hair. My mum tried to get it out, but it was so bad she had to cut it. That's when she noticed bald spots at the back of my head. I showed her my hairbrush, which was full of hair, and she took me to the doctor. They told me I had alopecia from the stress of the bullying. Not long after, I had to cut my hair short. I went from hair down to my waist to a jaw-length bob. I remember the hairdresser crying while cutting it because it was so long. Thankfully, the Spice Girls were popular then, so I just said I was copying Posh Spice.

Things kept getting worse. At one point, when I was at a friend's, her brother ran into the house and said, 'You need to leave. XXX is on their way with their parents to beat you up.' I called my parents, and they rushed to get me. Now adults – completely unrelated to the situation – were getting involved, all because of lies being spread about me.

My mum fought so hard to get the school to do something, but they didn't help. She tried contacting charities, lawyers, and even the police. Nobody seemed to care. I became a prisoner in my own home, too scared to go out. I refused to go to school, but the school wouldn't help. Instead, the education welfare officer threatened to send my parents to jail if I didn't go back. They begged for support, but it was like no one was listening.

While studying from home, I saw a TV show called *Kilroy* that was looking for people who had experienced bullying. I called in, and they asked me to be on the show. My mum didn't want me to go, but I felt like I needed

to. Surprisingly, it helped. The school saw the episode and agreed to let me take my exams in a separate room away from the other students. I was allowed to arrive and leave at different times to avoid any issues.

Even after I left school, the bullying didn't stop completely. When I was 20 and dating my first serious boyfriend, people would still slash his tyres or smash his car windows just because he was with me.

It finally ended when I moved away and cut ties with most people from my school. I kept in touch with a couple of people, but I didn't really have any 'real' friends. Even now, 25 years later, I find it hard to trust people. I've built walls around myself and don't let others get too close. I've blocked out a lot of the worst memories, mainly for my mental health because I don't think I could handle reliving it all.

Being bullied didn't ruin my life, but it changed me in ways I'm still dealing with. I used to think it made me stronger, but I realise now that it's made me closed off. I feel like I have to handle everything on my own because I don't trust others to be there for me. I still find it hard to make friends, but I'm content with the ones I have.

Being bullied as a teenager can leave deep scars, and for me, it has had a huge impact on how I approach relationships as an adult. Looking back, the bullying I experienced made it really hard for me to trust people, and that has stuck with me throughout my life. Even though the bullying ended long ago, it has shaped how I see friendships, and it's often in negative ways.

One of the biggest challenges I face is trusting people. When I was bullied, people I thought were my friends either turned against me or simply stood by and watched. This betrayal made me feel like I couldn't rely on anyone, and as a result, I find it really difficult to open up to new people. In my mind, I'm always waiting for the moment when they'll hurt me or leave me behind, just like what happened during those tough years at school. It's like I'm constantly guarded, always keeping my walls up to protect myself.

Because of this lack of trust, I find it hard to make new friends. I don't want to be in a position where I could get hurt again, so I often avoid getting too close to people. I'll be friendly, but I keep my distance. When people try to get to know me, I'm quick to put up barriers, only showing them a part of who I am. It's as if I'm testing them, waiting to see if they'll stick around long enough to prove they're trustworthy, but this approach means I miss out on potential friendships.

Another way the bullying has affected me is that I don't want to let people into my life. Back in school, being vulnerable was used against me. The bullies knew my weaknesses, and they exploited them. So now, I avoid sharing too much about myself. I've learned to keep my emotions and personal life private because I don't want to give anyone the chance to hurt me. When you don't let people in, it's hard to build meaningful relationships. I sometimes feel lonely because of this, but it's a defence mechanism I've developed to protect myself.

This fear of getting close to others doesn't just affect friendships, it also impacts romantic relationships. I struggle with being open and trusting in those, too. It's hard to believe that someone could truly care for me without eventually turning against me, so I tend to hold back. It's like I'm always expecting the worst, which makes it hard for relationships to grow. Even when people show me kindness and love, there's still that part of me that doesn't fully believe it.

In the end, being bullied as a teenager has made me cautious and closed-off in ways that have followed me into adulthood. I've missed out on forming deeper connections with people because I'm afraid of getting hurt again. It's something I'm still working through, but I've learned that healing from those experiences takes time. Even though it's tough, I try to remind myself that not everyone is going to hurt me, and that letting people in can lead to stronger, healthier relationships in the future.

*Name has been changed

Can bullying cause anxiety disorders?

By Jennifer Roblin

Childhood bullying can cause anxiety and trauma that carries over into later life and adulthood, often showing up as generalised or social anxiety, and/or lead to PTSD and panic attacks. The pain and distress victims experience impacts almost every aspect of their lives leaving them feeling lonely, isolated, vulnerable and anxious.

Bullying is victimising, shaming and humiliating, and a hurtful way to make someone feel rejected. When someone is bullied, they become ostracised, dismissed and isolated, and often go on to develop feelings of unworthiness, guilt and inadequacy.

Bullying can be a combination of emotional or physical abuse and it is not uncommon for someone who has been bullied as a child, to continue to be bullied long after their school days are over.

From an evolutionary perspective, we are wired to attach and belong to a tribe.

Our tribe would look out for us and keep us safe. It was not possible to hunt for food and keep a fire going continuously without the support of others in your tribe. Being ostracised was likely to lead to death.

Without an attachment to a tribe, our sense of belonging would be lost which can feel extremely scary, even in today's modern world. The nervous system activates the survival mechanisms of fight and flight when the emotions experienced are shame and hopelessness.

Bullying involves an imbalance of power between perpetrators and victims, where one perpetrator engages in physical or emotional abuse, and the victim is not able to defend themselves.

The most common anxiety disorders that may develop as a result of being bullied are:

- Generalised Anxiety Disorder (GAD)
- Social Anxiety Disorder
- Post Traumatic Stress Disorder (PTSD)
- Panic Attacks or Disorder

Generalised Anxiety Disorder (GAD)

Anxiety becomes a disorder if you are feeling intensely worried or fearful the majority of the time, and for an extended period of time. This is the most common form of anxiety and someone suffering with GAD may be inundated with worries and fears that distract them from their everyday lives. Anxiety can then have an impact on relationships, the ability to go to school or hold down employment, energy levels, concentration levels and sleep.

As a result of being bullied, you may have a constant dread that something else bad will happen to you. This may have an impact on their behaviour which could possibly make you more vulnerable to future bullying.

Social Anxiety Disorder

Social anxiety is an overwhelming feeling of intense fear and self-consciousness about being around other people. You may be worried that you will be ridiculed or humiliated or do something or act in a certain way that is embarrassing when in front of others. As a result, you may avoid public places or social gathering as you have an excessive fear of being judged or criticised.

Victims of bullying may develop a social anxiety disorder, especially if you were repeatedly shamed or publicly humiliated, and may believe that the humiliation and embarrassment you experienced previously will happen repeatedly.

Post Traumatic Stress Disorder (PTSD)

PTSD may occur after a particularly traumatic and terrifying event where some physical harm occurred, was witnessed or threatened, or after repeated abuse or bullying. PTSD will often result in flashbacks of past events and nightmares and may cause the sufferer to withdraw from others.

Panic Attacks or disorders

Someone with a panic disorder will regularly suffer with unprovoked and intense feelings of panic combined with the physical sensations that may include increased heart rate, shortness of breath, dizziness and often chest and/or stomach pain. These feelings of terror can be particularly scary when in the midst of an attack, as it can feel as if we have no control over what is happening to us and we can't properly take a breath.

When left untreated, panic attacks can lead sufferers to avoid going out or doing things you once enjoyed. You may have a constant worry that you will experience another attack so often choose to stay home where you feel safe

What can you do to overcome the long-term effects of bullying?

Firstly, understand that what happened to you was not your fault. Bullies often do what they do because they are struggling with something in their own lives, and they use the power imbalance to feel better about themselves. Bullies are often insecure and trying to fulfil a need for control in their own lives. Forgiving the bully can be a really helpful step in your recovery. If this is a stretch too far, then try and work on acceptance of what has happened to you, without guilt or shame. What skills would have helped you back then? If it was confidence, work on building up your confidence. If it was resilience, how can you build on this?

You may also find it helpful to work out what the coping strategies were that you used when you were younger, and see if you are still applying those same strategies today. Talking to a therapist could help you remove the negative emotions that you stored when you were bullied and help you rewrite your story to remove the 'victim' role.

You may possibly need to strengthen your social skills if they were not developed sufficiently when you were younger.

If you need further support

Overcoming anxiety is a journey that involves a combination of techniques and strategies.

While you can implement these tools independently, seeking the support of a mental health professional provides an additional level of guidance and assistance, and enables you and your child to get to the root cause of anxiety and negative thoughts.

Taking care of our mental health is an essential part of our overall wellbeing. Left unresolved, anxiety can spiral out of control and have a significant impact on relationships, work, school and family life.

It is my belief that no one needs to struggle with anxiety, we just need the strategies and techniques to overcome it.

17 November 2021

Design

Create a poster with advice on where to seek support for anxiety for bullying.

The above information is reprinted with kind permission from Better Your Life.
© 2024 Better Your Life

www.betteryourlife.co.uk

Devastating effects of bullying on children in the short and long-term

Bullying is often shrugged off as a 'normal' part of school life. But the effects of bullying on children can be devastating.

By Rebecca McCurdy

In the short term it can impact on victims' schooling and social life.

However, it can also have a lifelong impact on victims' mental health and how they view themselves, others and their education and future.

And it can impact the whole family as they struggle with supporting their child or sibling through the trauma.

The effects of bullying on children

Experts suggest that those who have been bullied are more likely to suffer from depression, low self-esteem and loneliness.

Here we outline some of the short and long-term effects of bullying.

1. Mental health

Bullied young people are more likely to suffer from a range of mental health concerns including depression and anxiety.

Bullies may focus on things that the child is already insecure about – their appearance or body image – which can heighten these concerns and lead to more serious mental health problems such as eating disorders or self-harm.

These issues may be hard for the young person to shake, even when the bullying stops and the mental health worries could stick with the child throughout their adult life.

And the Anti-Bullying Alliance suggests that bullying which occurs over a long period of time can significantly increase the impact bullying has on the victim.

2. Education

The effects of bullying on children may mean a struggle to focus on their school work, and grades could suffer as a result.

They are also more likely to avoid going to school or miss certain classes if they are worried about coming face-to-face with their tormentors.

As their self-esteem is impacted by the bullying, so too could their belief in their ability to complete projects or assignments and it may result in them not handing in work on time, or doing it to the best of their ability.

3. Friendships

Relationships can be impacted by bullying in various ways, for example, friends may even join in the bullying against you to protect themselves.

It can lead to trust issues for children as they struggle to know who their real friends are and who they can trust.

People who are bullied are more likely to have a hard time making friends or maintaining friendships or relationships.

Their self-worth could be so low that they may not think they are worthy of the lasting friendships.

4. Family life

When a child is being bullied, it can impact the whole family, including parents and siblings.

The child experiencing bullying may take their frustrations out on those who they feel comfortable around – often family.

And family members may struggle to understand why their child is being bullied and how to help them through the ordeal.

Anyone who witnesses bullying should report the incidents to a relevant authority, such as teachers, police or parents.

Scotland's anti-bullying service RespectMe offers guidance for young people who are experiencing bullying and their parents and teachers.

If you feel like the bullying you witnessed at school or online was a hate crime, you can also report it to Police Scotland via 101.

Childline support young people with any worries they may experience, including mental health and bullying.

They can be contacted confidentially on 0800 11 11.

The above information is reprinted with kind permission from The Courier.
© DC Thomson Co Ltd 2024

www.thecourier.co.uk

Study finds childhood bullying linked to distrust and mental health problems in adolescence

Teens who experience bullying and develop distrust of others are 3.5 times more likely to experience clinically significant mental health issues by age 17.

A new study, co-led by UCLA Health and the University of Glasgow, found that young teenagers who develop a strong distrust of other people as a result of childhood bullying are substantially more likely to have significant mental health problems as they enter adulthood compared to those who do not develop interpersonal trust issues.

The study, published in the journal Nature Mental Health, is believed to be the first to examine the link between peer bullying, interpersonal distrust, and the subsequent development of mental health problems, such as anxiety, depression, hyperactivity and anger.

Researchers used data from 10,000 children in the United Kingdom who were studied for nearly two decades as part of the Millennium Cohort Study. From these data, the researchers found that adolescents who were bullied at age 11 and in turn developed greater interpersonal distrust by age 14 were around 3.5 times more likely to experience clinically significant mental health problems at age 17 compared to those who developed less distrust.

The findings could help schools and other institutions to develop new evidence-based interventions to counter the negative mental health impacts of bullying, according to the study's senior author Dr George Slavich, who directs UCLA Health's Laboratory for Stress Assessment and Research.

Dr Slavish said: 'There are few public health topics more important than youth mental health right. In order to help teens reach their fullest potential, we need to invest in research that identifies risk factors for poor health and that translates this knowledge into prevention programs that can improve lifelong health and resilience.'

The findings come amid growing public health concerns about the mental health of youth. Recent studies by the US Centres for Disease Control and Prevention found that 44.2% of sampled high school students in the US reported being depressed for at least two weeks in 2021, with one in 10 students who were surveyed having reported attempted suicide that year.

In this new study, the researchers viewed these alarming trends from the perspective of Social Safety Theory, which hypothesises that social threats, such as bullying, impact mental health partly by instilling the belief that other people cannot be trusted, or that the world is an unfriendly, dangerous or unpredictable place.

Prior research has identified associations between bullying and mental and behavioural health issues among youth, including its impact on substance abuse, depression, anxiety, self-harm and suicidal thoughts. However, following youth over time, this study is the first to confirm the suspected pathway of how bullying leads to distrust and, in turn, mental health problems in late adolescence

The researchers explain that when people develop clinically significant mental health problems during the teenage years, it can increase their risk of experiencing both mental and physical health issues across the entire lifespan if left unaddressed.

In addition to interpersonal distrust, the authors examined if diet, sleep or physical activity also linked peer bullying with subsequent mental health problems. However, only interpersonal distrust was found to relate bullying to greater risk of experiencing mental health problems at age 17.

Dr Dimitris Tsomokos, co-author of the study from the University of Glasgow, said: 'Parents, teachers and researchers have known for a while that a sense of belonging in school and communities is crucial for children and adolescents, both in terms of academic performance and overall wellbeing. Our work provides evidence that a key reason for the breakdown of belonging is distrust, which develops over time and settles in – so to speak – in the form of negative social safety schemas. Distrust can emerge because of earlier experiences of bullying or due to other reasons, breaks down the sense of belonging, and degrades mental health.'

The study, 'Bullying fosters interpersonal distrust and degrades adolescent mental health as predicted by Social Safety Theory', is published in *Nature Mental Health*.

13 February 2024

The above information is reprinted with kind permission from The University of Glasgow.
© 2024 The University of Glasgow

www.tgla.ac.uk

Life after workplace bullying

How working with your brain can help return you to health and happiness.

By Jennifer Fraser Ph.D.

Key points

- The harm from being bullied in the workplace has a bad habit of lingering.
- When coaching clients who have bullied brains, I use a series of evidence-based practices to help them recover.
- Clients who have been bullied stop blaming themselves when they understand how betrayal trauma works.
- While we struggle to halt workplace bullying, we certainly can better self-regulate to protect our health and happiness.

Life after workplace bullying can be an ongoing torment as the target struggles to recover. For far too many, life after workplace bullying is one where illness and mental anguish continue to rule the day. The bullied brain needs to create a recovery plan. There are evidence-based steps to take in order to repair and recover after maltreatment in the workplace.

A number of my coaching clients have suffered from workplace bullying, and they are seeking techniques to return to their natural brain health. Before they get to the practices that are documented in science to help with a bullied brain, we address the confusion around why the bullying happened, and the frequent sense targets have that it was their own fault. Self-blame is a dead-end street on the road to recovery.

My clients want to know why as employees, they remained in a toxic environment and suffered repeat abuses. To overcome this obstacle to recovery, we must first recognise how bullying works in order to cast off its lingering harm.

Jennifer Freyd and Pamela Birrell detail the coping mechanism of blindness. They demonstrate the ways in which we fool ourselves into believing we are being treated fairly or that if we are maltreated, the fault lies with us. They show the ways in which we trick our own selves into trusting those who are utterly untrustworthy. Step one in the return to health and happiness after workplace bullying is to remove the blinders.

We put on blinders as a self-protective device

It's not blameworthy. Just a survival strategy. If the person who bullies you is powerful, influential, rules over others, and signs your paycheck, you may need to fool yourself into having faith in him or her. Any dependence, such as your livelihood or your benefits, puts you as an employee in a vulnerable position. You may well keep quiet about injustices, look the other way when wrongdoing occurs, and keep your eyes on the ground if the bullying individual targets others.

When you are in a workplace that has bullying, it is natural to find ways to cope until you can escape. However, as time passes, your sense of independence, your health, and your self-esteem are often eroded, which inevitably makes escape more difficult. Some of my clients were told in no uncertain terms by their doctors that they had to go on stress leave. Many of us, cowering behind our blinders, do not see just how damaging bullying is to our brains and bodies.

How can we remove the blinders and see workplace bullying without suffering a crisis?

Exercises I have my clients do are designed to keep a track record of the bullying incidents coupled with what their brain predicted in the moment. This is a practical application of Lisa Feldman Barrett's research on how we construct emotion. For instance, one client alerted his boss that his daughter was undergoing surgery, and he would have to shuttle back and forth from the hospital to work. Despite being up most of the night with his child's traumatic medical situation, he came to work on time the next day.

His brain predicted that his boss would care about him, be worried and empathic about his daughter, and recognise his effort during a difficult time to still focus on work. However, his boss did not speak to him all day. Didn't send him a note to check in. This startled and harmed his brain. Bullying by ignoring – communicating that someone's struggle and life are irrelevant, unworthy, and not even noticeable – is harmful. It creates doubt in the brain that then tries to find a reason for the lack of kindness and care. It's important not to let the brain choose 'it's your own fault' as a way to make sense of the cruelty.

When individuals who have suffered workplace bullying begin to list situations that occurred and record the way in which it baffled, hurt, and shocked their brains, they begin to see how going forward is a challenge, specifically for the brain.

The brain keeps wanting to figure out what went wrong, why it predicted incorrectly, and how it can better anticipate a malevolent world

The brain's goal is to make meaning from all the data perpetually bombarding it, and bullying behaviour can lead to confusion, as well as constantly looking back, trying to understand what happened and how such injustice and meanness could possibly occur. It's critically important for the brain to stop wading through what Michael Merzenich terms 'noise and chatter' as it tries to figure out what happened.

At this juncture, I have clients use mindfulness and visualisation to put a clear barrier between themselves and the past. If the brain can identify and write down instances of bullying, it helps the target to identify the destructive conduct as external and undeserved. This is a practical application of Dan Siegel's advice: 'Name it to tame it.' Bullying is a behaviour that someone else manifested. The brain must let it go, recognise through slow, deep breathing that it's safe, and set its considerable powers to the present moment full of opportunities.

Another exercise that helps the brain take stock of the crisis is to list on one side of the page the individuals who use bullying behaviour. On the other side of the page, list colleagues who are healthy, empathic, and who foreground social-emotional relationships. While some organisations are so rife with bullying that there may be quite a number who bully, inevitably, there are still more colleagues in the column of healthy and empathic connections. Frequently only one individual will appear on the bullying side, and this empowers the brain to recognise that bullying is an outlying and isolating conduct that breaks relationships down rather than making them strong.

Furthermore, the list shows the target that it is, in fact, the bully who is alone or in a small camp, while others are a community to which the target belongs. If the workplace is rife with bullying, then I have my client look at past communities to which they healthily belonged and then notice the unhealthy ones in which they were bullied.

Help targets self-regulate the seesaw of sympathetic and parasympathetic responses

Much of the mental and physical anguish that occurs when being bullied is linked to the repeat activation of the sympathetic stress response system. In a toxic workplace that lacks psychological safety, targets and even bystanders may have cortisol constantly being released and circulated in the brain and body. This cycle is very unhealthy.

I work with clients to learn that they can tip their response in the other direction and use aerobic exercise, being in nature, and practicing mindfulness to activate their parasympathetic system or, as scientists say, the 'rest-and-digest' system. This lowers cortisol, heart rate, and blood pressure and allows the brain and body time to repair and recover. While bullying might be out of your control, tilting the seesaw to rest and digest is within your own power.

24 October 2024

The above information is reprinted with kind permission from *Psychology Today*.
© 2024 Sussex Publishers, LLC

www.psychologytoday.com

Being bullied as an adult: breaking the silence

When most people hear the word 'bullying,' they often think of school playgrounds or teenagers in high school. But bullying doesn't end when you become an adult. It can happen in many settings, such as the workplace, in relationships, and even within families. Adult bullying is real, and it can be just as harmful as childhood bullying – sometimes even more so because people often don't talk about it.

Let's explore what adult bullying looks like, the emotional toll it takes, and how to confront it in different areas of life: the workplace, relationships, and families.

Workplace bullying

Many adults spend a significant portion of their time at work, and the workplace can sometimes turn into a toxic environment. Workplace bullying is when a colleague, manager, or even a group of people repeatedly belittle, humiliate, or intimidate someone. It's not just about disagreements or occasional harsh words; bullying in the workplace is persistent, harmful, and can cause long-lasting damage.

Bullying in the workplace can take many forms, such as:

- Undermining your work by constantly criticising or setting you up to fail.
- Spreading rumours about you or isolating you from others.
- Taking credit for your achievements while blaming you for any mistakes.
- Sabotaging your work, making it difficult for you to meet deadlines or succeed.

This kind of bullying can lead to stress, anxiety, and even depression. It can make you dread going to work every day, affecting your overall wellbeing and self-esteem. Sometimes, the bully might hold a position of authority, making it even harder to stand up for yourself.

Being bullied by a partner

In relationships, bullying can be difficult to recognise, especially if the behaviour develops gradually. Bullying by a partner often takes the form of emotional or psychological abuse, which can be just as damaging as physical violence. Your partner might:

- Control your behaviour, telling you who you can see, what you can wear, or where you can go.
- Constantly belittle you, criticising your appearance, intelligence, or abilities.
- Isolate you from friends and family, making you feel dependent on them alone.
- Manipulate you with guilt trips or silent treatment to get their way.

These behaviours aren't always easy to spot because they might be disguised as 'concern' or 'love.' For example, your partner might say they don't want you to go out with friends because they're worried about your safety, but if this happens repeatedly, it can be a form of control. Over time, this bullying can make you doubt your self-worth, convincing you that you deserve the mistreatment.

Being bullied by a family member

Family should be a source of love and support, but sadly, some people experience bullying from relatives. Family bullying can be especially painful because the people involved are supposed to be the ones who care for you the most. Whether it's a parent, sibling, or even an extended family member, this type of bullying can deeply affect your mental health and sense of identity.

Family bullying might include:

- Constant criticism or nitpicking about your choices, achievements, or lifestyle.
- Comparisons to other family members, making you feel inferior or inadequate.
- Manipulation or emotional blackmail, using guilt or obligations to control your behaviour.
- Threats of disownment or punishment if you don't conform to their expectations.

Because family relationships are often long-standing and emotionally complex, it can be incredibly hard to confront or escape from this kind of bullying. It can leave you feeling trapped, torn between loyalty to your family and the need to protect your own mental health.

The impact of adult bullying

Regardless of where it happens – at work, in a relationship, or within your family – being bullied as an adult can have devastating effects. It can make you feel helpless, trapped, or like you have no one to turn to. Many adults don't speak up about being bullied because they fear being judged, or they might feel ashamed, thinking they should be able to handle it on their own.

The emotional impact of bullying can include:

- Anxiety: Constantly feeling on edge, worrying about how the bully might act next.
- Depression: Losing interest in things you once enjoyed, feeling sad or hopeless.
- Low self-esteem: Beginning to believe the cruel things the bully says about you.
- Physical symptoms: Stress from bullying can lead to headaches, trouble sleeping, or even more serious health problems.

Chapter 3: Stamping Out Bullying

Top 5 tips to handle bullying

By Beatrice Welch

Bullying is a serious issue that affect many people, particularly children and teenagers in school with one in five students report being bullied. Handling bullying can be challenging but here are five top tips to help you handle this issue.

1. Ignore the bully

Make every effort to ignore the threats made by the bully, act as if you weren't aware of them, and walk off to a safe location. Ignoring the bully will demonstrate that you don't care and they will soon lose interest in bothering you and give up. It's a good idea to practice ways of ignoring the bully such as sending someone a text on your mobile phone or appearing uninterested. If you have friends around, the bully will be less likely to approach you, so make sure you stick together during the school day.

2. Stand up for yourself

Bullies usually target shy and vulnerable people so you should try to act brave and confident around the bully. Tell them to stop in a loud voice and calmly walk away. You could also receive support from your friends, ask them to stand around the bully with you and say stop too. Since the bully is now surrounded by others who are also demanding at them to stop, this likely is going to scare them away.

3. Don't retaliate

It's important to stay calm and not react to the bully by hitting, kicking or pushing back. Fighting back will not only satisfy the bully and provoke them to continue, but it could also be dangerous and lead to someone getting injured.

4. Don't show any emotions

It is natural to feel anger and distressed by the bully, but that's what bullies want, they are expecting to thrive on this reaction. So, it is important to show no emotion when interacting with the bully. Since this can be difficult, it could be beneficial to practise some 'cool down' techniques. For example, some children find that counting to ten, taking deep breaths or simply walking away can be useful.

5. Seek support

It is very important to seek help if you are bullied, you should discuss what is going on with someone you trust, such as a parent, friend or teacher. It could be helpful to receive support from school because bullies are more likely to stop once the teachers find out because they fear punishment from their parents. Sharing your experience with friends can provide emotional support, and they may be able to help you stand up to the bully. However, if you don't feel comfortable speaking to someone you know, you can always reach out to a support service. The National Bullying Helpline is an anonymous resource that offers free online assistance to anyone experiencing bullying-related problems. If you would prefer to talk to someone in person, Little Lives UK offers children the opportunity to talk with professional therapists about their concerns in free counselling sessions.

The above information is reprinted with kind permission from Little Lives UK.
© 2024 Little Lives UK

www.littlelives.org.uk

I'm a bully – and I want to stop

How to get help when YOU'RE the bully…

There's a lot of advice and support out there for people who are being bullied, but there's very little help for those who are doing the bullying. If you're here, then we want to say well done. You've made the first step towards getting help and making positive changes to your behaviour.

How do I know if I'm a bully?

It's not always easy to know if you're a bully. You might think that the things you say are just 'banter', or that you're only joking around and don't mean any harm. Try to think how you'd feel if you were in the other person's shoes. Be honest.

It's not nice to think of ourselves in a negative light. We try to avoid admitting our faults and even make excuses for our negative behaviour, even when we know deep down that we're in the wrong.

Ask yourself these questions and answer honestly. Do you ever:

- Repeatedly upset someone, perhaps a classmate, sibling or friend?
- Find it difficult to empathise with others? This can be difficult to see in yourself so you can ask friends or family for their thoughts.
- Feel like you're at your strongest when you're around insecure people?
- Deliberately pick on someone to make yourself feel better?
- Make passive aggressive comments?
- Get aggressive with others?
- Spread rumours or spill secrets?
- Deliberately isolate people?
- Send unpleasant messages or make mean comments on social media?

If you've answered 'yes' to many of these questions, this is an indication that you need to pay more attention to how you treat others. Negative behaviour can cause a lot of damage which is why it's so important to be considerate and careful with your words and actions.

Why do I bully?

There are lots of reasons why a person might bully. It's often complex but, more often than not, a bully has some trauma or pain going on in their own life. It can help to understand why you are bullying. You may be experiencing:

- Family issues such as a divorce or arguments in the home.
- Alcohol or drug abuse issues.
- The death of a relative.
- Issues with siblings.
- Being bullied yourself. People who are bullied can sometimes become a bully themselves.
- Low self-esteem.
- Insecure relationships with family, friends, or both.
- Pressure from peers – feeling as if you must behave in a certain way to keep your friends.

Once you identify your triggers, you can look for healthier ways to deal with your feelings and emotions. Changing behaviour patterns often takes time and practice, so don't beat yourself up if you slip-up occasionally.

It can also help to understand the impact bullying can have on others. Bullying can take its toll on a person's mental health and self-esteem. It can be incredibly isolating, upsetting and scary. The damage caused by bullying can impact a person for years to come or, worse, drive them to harm themselves.

Getting help

There's no shame in reaching out for support. You have identified areas where you need help with your behaviour and that's something to be applauded. You're taking ownership and taking steps to make yourself a better person.

You don't have to do this alone – talk to a parent, teacher or adult you trust to get help. Or speak to one of our trained counsellors on the Hidden Strength app. Together, you can look for different ways to channel your frustrations, stress and anger.

17 November 2021

The above information is reprinted with kind permission from Hidden Strength.
© 2024 Hidden Strength Holdings Ltd

www.hiddenstrength.com

How to stop bullying others: 7 practical tips

We recently found that 1 in 2 people have bullied another person at least once. Bullying is one of the biggest issues currently affecting young people and we believe that we can overcome it, if we start to think differently about how we resolve things.

We believe that nobody is ever a bully. They may be bullying somebody, which is a behaviour, but it isn't who they are as people. Our experts have compiled together seven practical tips which are designed to help you stop bullying others by enabling you to understand your behaviours better and equipping you to resolve them in more effective ways.

1. You are not a bully

First and foremost, stop labelling yourself as a bully. It isn't productive and will not benefit you. You may be bullying another person but that does not mean you are a bully. It is a behaviour and not your identity.

Nobody is born a bully, in fact – bullies don't technically even exist. We know that people often exhibit bullying behaviours when they are going through stress or trauma, are being bullied themselves or when they have particularly low self-esteem and confidence.

2. Understand why

Our research shows that there are a variety of reasons why people bully others. Bullying is a learned behaviour and is often used as a coping mechanism for a stressful situation. Common examples could include being bullied by somebody else, abuse, a traumatic situation or a stressful home life.

Have you ever been so stressed you've ended up snapping at your parents or your best mate? We all have, pretty much. When you're in that headspace, it's difficult to control it – but if you acknowledge you're stressed, you can start to change your reactions so that you become less snappy – or you can just warn people to give you some space for a while.

In addition, we also know that some people bully others because they may feel competitive towards them or they may not fully understand an element about them. Once you are able to gain an understanding as to why you are motivated to bully others, this will give you hugely valuable insight.

3. Seek a resolve

Once you have identified the source of your behaviour, it is important to find a productive way in which you can resolve the situation. If you find this difficult, we would recommend speaking with an adult who you trust.

Alternatively, you can contact us or give our friends at Childline a call on 0800 11 11. Believe us when we tell you that you are deserving of support.

4. Reprogram your stress

What is the one thing that we all have in common? Stress. We all feel it, but it's important to recognise stress and deal with it accordingly. By that, we mean - don't store it up and let it fester, as it can have significant impacts on your mood and health. Give our Stress Reprogramming system a try.

5. Speak about it

You'd be surprised at how powerful it can be to just sit down with somebody who you trust and talk about everything that is bothering you. A problem shared, really can be a problem halved. It may be worth buddying up and going through our Stress Reprogramming exercise with somebody who you trust.

6. Is it a good strategy?

Pulling somebody else down will never, ever take you any higher. Using bullying as a coping mechanism for something stressful in your life is only going to make things worse; not just for you but also for the person who is at the receiving end of the bullying.

7. Understand the impact

To you, it may not seem serious, but to another person, the impact could be significant. For every 10 people who are bullied, three of them will self-harm, one will go on to have a failed suicide attempt and one will develop an eating disorder. Additionally, we know that people who have been bullied, on average, achieve lower grades and therefore the bullying could reduce their future career prospects.

Above everything, we would encourage you to please speak to somebody and seek the support available. This could be a Ditch the Label Mentor who will offer non judgmental advice and support.

28 April 2022

The above information is reprinted with kind permission from Ditch the Label.
© 2024 Ditch the Label Youth Charity.

www.ditchthelabel.org

Scientists find 'potential breakthrough' to stop bullying in schools

New method can help create more pro-victim bystanders and 'anti-bullying climate' in schools.

By Vishwam Sankaran

A new way of tackling bullying trialled among students in South Korea could be a potential game-changer in creating an 'anti-bullying climate' in schools, scientists say.

Bullying, or peer victimisation, is a worldwide crisis across schools that can devastate victims, likely leading to depression, anxiety, and self-harm.

Researchers have attempted to tackle bullying previously by focusing on ways to change individual students' behaviour.

However, educational psychologists, including those from Korea University, say such past interventions have been 'largely unsuccessful'.

The latest study, published recently in the journal American Psychology, trialled a new way of tackling bullying that lays focus on teachers creating an 'anti-bullying climate' in classrooms.

Psychologists equipped teachers with professional development experience to establish a highly supportive classroom climate.

They attempted to enable with this method the emergence of pro-victim student bystanders during bullying episodes in classrooms.

In the new study, scientists attempted to create a social environment that encourages more students to defend victims.

Researchers looked at a group of 24 experienced, full-time physical education teachers in Seoul, including 15 men and nine women teachers who taught adolescent students.

The study assessed two classes taught by each teacher, totalling to 1,178 students across 48 classes.

Over a semester spanning 18 weeks, the teachers were sorted into two groups – one that had no intervention, and another taught the new approach to prevent bullying called 'autonomy-supportive teaching.'

In this new approach, teachers cultivated a classroom environment for students emphasising caring, egalitarian values, minimising hierarchy, conflict, and competition.

The students reported their perceived teacher autonomy support, classmates' autonomy support, adoption of the defender role, and the bullying they experienced at the beginning, middle, and end of an 18-week semester.

Researchers found that the new method led to the emergence of pro-victim peer bystanders and 'sharply reduced victimisation'.

'Unlike largely unsuccessful past interventions that focused mainly on individual students, our randomised control trial intervention substantially reduced bullying and victimization,' scientists wrote in the study.

They say focusing on individual students is likely to be ineffective, without first changing the social climate in classrooms that reinforces bullying.

'In the classrooms of these teachers, bystanders supported the victims because the classroom climate supported the bystanders,' researchers added.

30 March 2023

The above information is reprinted with kind permission from *The Independent*.
© independent.co.uk 2024

www.independent.co.uk

Stamping out bullying

Bullying is a major issue in schools throughout the UK. It can happen in many forms – verbal, physical, social, or online (also known as cyberbullying) – and it can have long-lasting effects on those who experience it. Young people who are bullied often struggle with low self-esteem, anxiety, depression, and poor performance at school. For many, bullying makes school feel like an unsafe place. However, it is possible to put an end to bullying, and everyone in the school community has a role to play. Here are some ways to eradicate bullying from schools and create a positive, safe environment for all students.

1. Encouraging a culture of kindness and respect

The foundation for preventing bullying lies in building a school culture that values kindness, empathy, and respect. When students feel valued and understood, they are less likely to bully others or tolerate bullying. Schools can promote this culture by setting clear expectations for behaviour. This means that students must know the importance of treating everyone with respect, regardless of differences in appearance, background, or abilities.

Teachers can help by incorporating lessons on empathy into their classrooms. For example, students can participate in activities that encourage them to understand the feelings of others or think about how they would feel in certain situations.

2. Reporting bullying without fear

Many students who experience bullying hesitate to speak up. They may worry that reporting the bullying will make them a target for further abuse, or they might fear that no one will take their claims seriously. For bullying to be stopped, it must be reported immediately. Schools must have systems in place that allow students to report bullying safely and without fear of retaliation.

This could involve creating anonymous reporting tools, such as a suggestion box or an online reporting system. Schools should also make it clear that anyone who reports bullying will be supported. Teachers and staff must respond quickly and effectively to reports, ensuring that students feel heard and that the bullying behaviour is addressed promptly.

3. Raising awareness through anti-bullying campaigns

Awareness is key to preventing bullying. Schools can organise anti-bullying campaigns to educate students about what bullying is, how it affects people, and why it must be stopped. Anti-bullying week, held every November, is a great opportunity for schools to focus on this issue through assemblies, workshops, and activities that engage students.

These campaigns can also highlight different types of bullying, including the often less visible forms, such as emotional manipulation and exclusion. The more students understand about the impact of bullying, the more likely they are to recognise when it is happening, whether to themselves or others, and to take action to stop it.

4. Empowering bystanders to take action

Bystanders play a crucial role in whether bullying continues or stops. In many cases, bullying is witnessed by others who may feel uncomfortable but do not intervene. This could be because they are unsure what to do, fear becoming targets themselves, or think that someone else will step in.

Schools need to teach students how to be 'upstanders' rather than passive bystanders. Upstanders are individuals who take action to support someone who is being bullied, whether by comforting them, standing up to the bully, or getting help from a teacher. If more students felt empowered to step in when they see bullying, it would be much harder for bullying to thrive.

5. Teaching conflict resolution and social skills

In many cases, bullying arises because of unresolved conflicts or misunderstandings. Teaching students how to handle disagreements peacefully and constructively can reduce the likelihood of bullying occurring. Schools can offer lessons on conflict resolution, problem-solving, and communication skills, helping students learn how to express their feelings and resolve disputes without resorting to hurtful behaviour.

Additionally, social skills training can help students who may be struggling to form friendships or fit in, making them less vulnerable to becoming bullies or victims of bullying. By helping all students develop emotional intelligence, schools can create a more harmonious environment.

6. Involving parents and the wider community

Bullying doesn't just happen in school. It can also occur online, on social media, or in other parts of a student's life. That's why it's important for parents and the wider community to be involved in the fight against bullying. Schools can work closely with parents to ensure they understand the signs of bullying and know how to support their children if they are involved, whether as victims or bullies.

Parents can also help by monitoring their children's online behaviour, talking to them about the importance of kindness and respect, and being proactive in addressing any issues they notice.

7. Enforcing a strong anti-bullying policy

Finally, every school in the UK must have a strong anti-bullying policy in place. This policy should clearly define what constitutes bullying, outline the consequences for bullying, and explain the procedures for reporting and addressing it. A transparent and well-enforced policy shows students that bullying is taken seriously and will not be tolerated.

The policy should be shared with students, staff, and parents, so everyone knows what to expect if bullying occurs. When students see that their school is committed to preventing bullying, they are more likely to feel safe and confident in reporting it.

Together, we can stop bullying and make schools a better place for everyone.

What should I do if I'm being bullied?

If you're being bullied, it's important to know that you're not alone, and there are steps you can take to address the situation. Here's what you can do if you're being bullied.

1. Talk to someone you trust

One of the most important things you can do is talk to someone about what's happening. This could be a parent, teacher, school counsellor, or even a close friend. It can feel scary to open up, but it's essential to let someone know what you're going through. They can provide support, offer advice, or even take action on your behalf. Keeping it all to yourself can make the situation feel more overwhelming than it really is.

2. Stay calm and don't react

Bullies often want to get a reaction out of you because it makes them feel more powerful. As hard as it is, try not to react with anger or fear in front of them. Stay calm, walk away, and avoid giving them the response they're looking for. By not letting them see that they're bothering you, you take away some of their control.

3. Save evidence

If you're being bullied online, it's crucial to save any messages, texts, or comments. Screenshots or saved conversations can serve as evidence when you report the bullying to an adult or authority figure. Even if it's happening in person, try to write down the details – what happened, when, where, and who was involved. Having a record can help when you need to prove what's been happening.

4. Report the bullying

Most schools have policies to handle bullying, so report the behaviour to a teacher, counsellor, or principal. If the bullying happens online, report it on the platform where it's occurring (such as social media) as most websites have ways to report harassment. Speaking up might feel daunting, but schools and online platforms have systems in place to help protect you.

5. Build your support network

Surround yourself with friends and people who care about you. Bullies often target people they perceive as isolated, so staying close to supportive friends can make a huge difference. These friends can help you feel less alone and more confident, and they can stand up for you if they witness any bullying.

6. Focus on self-care

Being bullied can take a toll on your mental and emotional health. Make sure you take time for yourself to relax, de-stress, and do things you enjoy. Whether it's playing a sport, watching your favourite shows, or talking to a friend, self-care can help you stay strong. If you're feeling really overwhelmed, talking to a therapist or counsellor can also be a great way to manage your feelings.

7. Don't blame yourself

It's important to remember that bullying is not your fault. Bullies often act out because of their own insecurities or issues, and their behaviour says more about them than it does about you. You are valuable and worthy of respect, regardless of what a bully might say or do.

8. Stay safe

If you ever feel physically unsafe or threatened, it's crucial to remove yourself from the situation immediately and seek help. Your safety is the top priority. Tell a teacher, parent, or any adult in authority if you feel like the bullying is putting you in danger.

In conclusion

Dealing with bullying is tough, but there are ways to stand up against it. By speaking up, staying calm, and building your support system, you can take control of the situation. Remember, bullying doesn't define you, and there are people who care about you and want to help. Don't hesitate to reach out – you deserve to be treated with kindness and respect.

Where can I find help?

Below are some telephone numbers, email addresses and websites of agencies or charities that can offer support or advice if you, or someone you know, needs it.

Childline
Helpline: 0800 1111
www.childline.org.uk

Anti-Bullying Alliance
www.anti-bullyingalliance.org.uk

National Bullying Helpline
Helpline: 0300 323 0169
www.nationalbullyinghelpline.co.uk

Shout
Text: 85258
www.giveusashout.org

Respect Me (Scotland's Anti-Bullying Service)
www.respectme.org.uk

Children 1st Scotland
Helpline: 08000 28 22 33
www.children1st.org.uk

Ditch The Label
www.ditchthelabel.org

Coram Child Law Advice
Family Line: 0300 330 5480
www.childlawadvice.org.uk

Acas (for workplace bullying)
Helpline 0300 123 1100
www.acas.org.uk

If you, or someone you know is being bullied, speak to a trusted adult for help.

To see more from the Government on the laws around bullying please visit: www.gov.uk/bullying-at-school

Remember, some forms of bullying are illegal and should be reported to the police. These include:
- violence or assault
- theft
- repeated harassment or intimidation, for example name calling, threats and abusive phone calls, emails or text messages
- hate crimes

Call 999 if you or someone else is in immediate danger.

issues: Anti-Bullying — Chapter 3: Stamping Out Bullying

Further Reading/ Useful Websites

Useful websites

www.anti-bullyingalliance.org.uk

www.artefactmagazine.com

www.betteryourlife.co.uk

www.ditchthelabel.org

www.hiddenstrength.com

www.independent.co.uk

www.littlelives.org.uk

www.metro.co.uk

www.ons.gov.uk

www.psychologytoday.com

www.strengthrestored.co.uk

www.tgla.ac.uk

www.theconversation.com

www.thecourier.co.uk

www.theguardian.com

www.yougov.co.uk

Further Reading

The Bullied Brain: Heal Your Scars and Restore Your Health by Jennifer Fraser: https://bulliedbrain.com/the-bullied-brain

Wonder R. J. Palacio

We Are All Made of Molecules Susin Nielsen

The Weight of Water Sarah Crossan

The Teenage Guide to Friends Nicola Morgan

Lord of the Flies William Golding

Glossary

Baiting
A method of provocation. To intentionally make someone angry by doing or saying things to annoy them.

Banter
An exchange of teasing remarks.

Bullying
A form of aggressive behaviour used to intimidate someone. It can be inflicted both physically and mentally (psychologically).

Communications Act 2003
The Communications Act 2003 governs the Internet, e-mail, mobile phone calls and text messaging. This means that it is an offence to send messages or other matter that are 'grossly offensive or of an indecent, obscene or menacing character', whether the targeted person actually sees the message or not.

Cyberbullying
Cyberbullying is when technology is used to harass, embarrass or threaten to hurt someone. A lot is done through social networking sites such as Facebook and X. Bullying via mobile phones is also a form of cyberbullying. With the use of technology on the rise, there are more and more incidents of cyberbullying.

Discrimination
Unfair treatment of someone because of the group/class they belong to.

Emotional Abuse
Emotional abuse refers to a victim being verbally attacked, criticised and put down. Following frequent exposure to this abuse, the victim's mental wellbeing suffers as their self-esteem is destroyed and the perpetrator's control over them increases. They may suffer from feelings of worthlessness, believing that they deserve the abuse or that if they were to leave the abuser they would never find another partner. A victim way also have been convinced by their abuser that the abuse is their fault. The abuser can use these feelings to manipulate the victim.

Flaming
Flaming involves using extremely offensive language in order to get into online arguments or fights.

Harassment
Usually persistent (but not always), a behaviour that is intended to cause distress and offence. It can occur on the school playground, in the workplace and even at home.

Homophobic bullying
Homophobia is the fear or hatred of people who are attracted to the same sex as themselves (e.g., disliking lesbians, gay men and bisexuals). This form of bullying is slightly different because of the personal motivation that drives it, in this case being directed at someone who is gay, lesbian or thought to be by others.

Non-Verbal abuse
Can be thought of as a kind of 'psychological warfare' because instead of using spoken words or direct physical violent behaviour, this form of abuse involves the use of mimicry (teasing someone by mimicking them), offensive gestures or body language.

Physical abuse
Physical abuse involves the use of violence or force against a victim and can including hitting, slapping, kicking, pushing, strangling or other forms of violence. Physical assault is a crime and the police have the power to protect victims, but in a domestic violence situation it can sometimes take a long time for the violence to come to light. Some victims are too afraid to go to the police, believe they can reform the abuser (who they may still love), or have normalised their abusive situation and do not realise they can get help.

Racist bullying
Targeting a person because of their race, colour or beliefs. There is a difference between racism and racial harassment: racial harassment refers to words and actions that are intentionally said/done to make the target feel small and degraded due to their race or ethnicity.

Sexual bullying
This includes a range of behaviours such as sexualised name-calling and verbal abuse, mocking someone's sexual performance, ridiculing physical appearance, criticising sexual behaviour, spreading rumours about someone's sexuality or about sexual experiences they have had or not had, unwanted touching and physical assault. Sexual bullying is behaviour which is repeated over time and intends to victimise someone by using their gender, sexuality or sexual (in)experience to hurt them.

Social media
Media which are designed specifically for electronic communication. 'Social networking' websites allow users to interact using instant messaging, share information, photos and videos and ultimately create an online community. Examples include Facebook, LinkedIn and micro-blogging site X.

Troll/Troller/Trolling
Troll is Internet slang for someone who intentionally posts something online to provoke a reaction. The idea behind the trolling phenomenon is that it is about humour, mischief and, some argue, freedom of speech; it can be anything from a cheeky remark to a violent threat. However, sometimes these Internet pranks can be taken too far, such as a person who defaces Internet tributes site, causing the victim's family further grief.

Verbal abuse
Spoken words out loud intended to cause harm, such as suggestive remarks, jokes or name calling.

Index

A
actions
 for bullies 36, 37
 if bullied 35, 40
 in schools 16–17, 38
adult targets of bullying 6–7, 8, 32–33, 34
age 5–6
anti-bullying climate 38
anxiety disorders 28–29

B
brain, effect on 14–15
buildings, size and shape 16–17
bullies
 reasons for bullying 12–13, 36, 37
 support for 36, 37
bystanders 38, 39

C
children 6–8, 9–11, 30, 31 see also schools
cyberbullying see online bullying

D
disabilities 5

E
education, effect on 5, 30
emotional bullying 4

F
family
 bullying within 7, 34
 changes within 12–13
 effect of bullying on target's 30
forgiveness 23, 24–25
friendships 3, 13, 22–23, 26–27, 30

G
gender 5, 8

H
help
 for bullies 36, 37
 for targets of bullying 20–21, 29, 33, 35, 40

I
impacts of bullying see also personal experience
 adults 6–7, 34
 children 6–7, 30, 31
 health and wellbeing 3, 14–15, 28–29, 30, 31
indirect bullying 4
in-person bullying 9–11
intent to cause hurt 2–3

M
masculinity 13
mental health 14–15, 28–29, 30, 31

O
online bullying 3, 4, 7–8, 9–10
online support 20–21

P
panic attacks 29
partners 7, 34
personal experience 18–21, 22–23, 24–25, 26–27
physical bullying 4, 7–8
power and powerlessness 3, 12–13
prevalence of bullying 5, 6–8
PTSD (post traumatic stress disorder) 18–19, 29

R
repetition 2–3
reporting 11, 30, 39

S
safer spaces 16–17
schools
 dealing with bullying 11, 16–17, 38, 39
 prevalence of bullying 5, 7
self-esteem 12, 13
SEN (special educational needs) 5
sexuality 13
shame 18, 21
social bullying 4

T
targets as bullies 12
TikTok 20–21
trauma, dealing with 18–21
trust 27, 31
types of bullying 2–3, 4

V
verbal bullying 4

W
workplace bullying 4, 32–33, 34